Mrs. Alexander

The Executor

Volume III

Mrs. Alexander

The Executor
Volume III

ISBN/EAN: 9783337053314

Printed in Europe, USA, Canada, Australia, Japan

Cover: Foto ©Andreas Hilbeck / pixelio.de

More available books at **www.hansebooks.com**

THE EXECUTOR

A Novel

BY

MRS. ALEXANDER

AUTHOR OF

THE WOOING O'T,' 'WHICH SHALL IT BE?' 'THE FRERES,' 'HER DEAREST FOE,'
AND 'LOOK BEFORE YOU LEAP.'

IN THREE VOLUMES

VOLUME III.

LONDON

RICHARD BENTLEY & SON, NEW BURLINGTON ST.

Publishers in Ordinary to Her Majesty the Queen

1883

Printed by R. & R. CLARK, *Edinburgh*

THE EXECUTOR.

CHAPTER I.

As she had told Brooke, Stasie was in the highest spirits at the prospect of her visit to Lady Pearson.

She anticipated a complete change of "scenery, decorations, and actors." This was enough to create great expectations, but beyond and above this was a sense of joyous freedom, of relief, in the certainty that for a fortnight at all events, she was safe from hearing or seeing Kharapet.

It was ungrateful and unreasonable to feel thus, she told herself, for nothing could be more irreproachable and brotherly than the Syrian's conduct. He certainly looked ill, though he made no complaint; this was a silent protest with which she could not quarrel, but it worried and oppressed her. Now she was speeding away from vexations, with an eternity of at least fifteen days' light and liberty before her !

Beyond so large a space of time what young creature would care to look ? especially one of Stasie's joyous temperament, ready as she was to believe all things, and hope all things.

The line to Portsmouth is sufficiently pretty to interest and amuse so inexperienced a traveller. When she had exhausted Aunt Clem's newspaper she gave it to a gruff old lady opposite, who relaxed towards her, and went so far as to ask, in condemnatory tones, if she expected any one to meet her, adding that in her day (the old lady's) young women did not run about the world alone ! To which Stasie replied that the world being much better nowadays, they could do so with impunity.

It was near sunset when they reached their journey's end, and Stasie quickly recognised Lady Pearson's dignified and portly figure, attended by a grave, severely respectable "man out of livery," as the train stopped alongside the platform. She was speedily almost, if not altogether, in her ladyship's would-be maternal arms.

"So good of you to come on such short notice, my dear Miss Verner!"

"And still better of you to ask me," cried Stasie, accepting an offered kiss. " I was feeling that I wanted change when your invitation came, and this is a delightful one!"

Stasie's luggage was soon disentangled, and given in charge to Lady Pearson's man. While her hostess explained that her daughter's carriage awaited them, as Sir Frederic did not think it worth while to bring their own from London. "You do not know my daughter, Mrs. Dalzell," continued Lady Pearson. "She is very bright and pleasant, rather like Van; you will be sure to like her," etc. etc. " If you are not very tired we will go round by the pier." Stasie was not tired, and much enjoyed the view as they drove round the common. The sea lay sleeping, bathed in gold by the grand blazonment of the setting sun, now low down on the horizon, beyond the richly-wooded gentle slopes of the Isle of Wight, touched with light on its western curves, shaded off into soft darkness to the east. Nearer, one of the round forts which rises from the water, was tinged with rich yellow light, in which the majestic form of a "man-of-war" at anchor showed black and solid her masts and rigging like a clear photograph against the vivid sky.

Men were playing cricket on the common—a wide stretch of green (very brown green at this season) bordered by houses of various styles and sizes at one side and the sea at the other, its shore line broken by a quaint old white fortification called the Castle. Children also disported themselves there on donkeys ; gay dresses, red and blue uniforms, added colour to the scene ; while the shining water was dotted with small craft, and white sails. Life—abundant joyous life—was everywhere, and Stasie felt as if a fresh stream of vitality had been suddenly poured into her own veins.

"How charming, how lovely !" she exclaimed, her eyes sparkling.

"Yes, it is very nice," returned Lady Pearson. "There is really nothing to speak of as regards scenery ; but the sea, and the people and ships and things make up a pleasant whole. I like Southsea in the autumn—it is better still in October—when most of the London people are gone. We generally come here. My son-in-law, Colonel Dalzell, has an appointment here, and I am glad to be with my daughter."

"Yes, of course," said Stasie with warm acquiescence. "If I had a mother I do not think I could bear to leave her, even for a husband."

"Ah! my dear Miss Verner, that is not the usual view young ladies take of their mothers," returned Lady Pearson, smiling, "though they do not always find they change for the better."

"Well, I suppose it is because I have never known one that I have always longed so much for a mother!"

"I am sure you would be a charming daughter to any mother," cried Lady Pearson with effusion. "But you would never want sympathising friends under any circumstances! I am glad you like Southsea, my dear, and as we have taken our present abode for a couple of months, I hope you will prolong your visit. Your aunt cannot hope to monopolise a girl like *you.*"

"You are very good," murmured Stasie, colouring with pleasure, and as usual responding to the voice of the charmer. Praise was very sweet to her, not altogether from vanity, though this had its share, but because kindness, approval, love were so dear to her heart. She longed always for affection, sympathy, comprehension, and keenly felt the loneliness of her position at times. Lady Pearson was a dear delightful appreciative woman, and nothing but a growing recognition of the fitness of things kept her impulsive companion from throwing her arms round her and telling her so.

Altogether Stasie's anticipations of pleasure seemed likely to be fulfilled.

As she was so fresh, and there was plenty of time, they took a second turn on the sea road, and watched the sun sink, leaving an exquisite flush of crimson fading into purple and saffron, and finally dying out into a warm gray as they drove slowly along. Lady Pearson returned the salutes of men in and out of uniform, and hand-kissings from ladies and children at nearly every step.

At length the horses' heads were turned towards Eastney, and stopped at one of a row of tall stone houses with large bay windows. The door stood open, giving a view of the hall beyond, and an array of hats and plaids hanging on the wall in delightful country fashion.

"You must take us just as we are, dear," said Lady Pearson, as they ascended the steps. "This is a mere lodging-house, and we have only brought my maid and Lennard; but the people are very obliging, and do not cook badly. Lennard," to the servant, "tell the coachman to drive to the pier, and wait for the seven o'clock boat from Ryde. Mrs. Dalzell said she would return by it."

The drawing-room seemed handsome and comfortable to Stasie's partial eyes, and the view out across the Solent to the island was delightful. Then the kindly, smiling hostess inducted Stasie into her special apartment, which was above the drawing-room, with the same outlook, and nearly as large. A nice writing-table and easy-chair in the window, a cheval glass, and sundry luxuries to which Stasie was not accustomed, made it seem quite grand to her. Her box was conveniently placed and freed from strap and cover, while a neat, composed young woman stood by ready to unlock and unpack it.

It was all delightful, and when Lady Pearson, with many injunctions to the maid to save Miss Verner all possible trouble, when that functionary asked with bated breath for the young lady's keys, it began to dawn on Stasie's charmed senses that she was something of a personage.

"She is *the* very most delightful girl I ever met in my life!" said Lady Pearson to her husband, when they met in the drawing-room, before their guest descended. "Handsome, well-bred, though not conventional, and so sweet and intelligent! She would be a charming wife for any man, independent of her fortune."

"Hum," returned the General. "How much do they say she is worth?"

"From what I can gather, something like forty thousand pounds."

"Well, take it at half what you hear—and that is not a bad sum to start a young couple well."

"Mrs. Dalton told me, and she is sure to know. She is quite intimate with Lady Elizabeth Wyatt. That handsome Eastern who is always there, I forget his name——"

"Yes, I know, the executor," interrupted Sir

Frederic. "Harding is the acting man, I think; and, if I don't wrong him, he'll make the estate pay for the trouble it gives him."

"It would really be a mercy to marry that dear girl to some nice, good young man as soon as possible. She is terribly alone, and at the mercy of designing people."

"Eh! my Lady," exclaimed the General, laughing, "you go ahead at a swinging pace! I suppose you have a pattern young man in your eye?"

"I have indeed, Sir Frederic! Oh, you need not laugh; but I never saw a girl I should so like for a daughter-in-law."

"Don't be in a hurry! and be sure about the rhino."

"Sh—sh!" said Lady Pearson, whose seat commanded the door, shaking her fan at her husband, as Stasie entered, looking very fair and graceful, in a white dress with a deep red sash, and a bouquet of damask roses.

Sir Frederic met her with a pleasant mixture of fatherly kindness and chivalrous courtesy, and expressed his pleasure at receiving her at his house. Stasie was delighted with him, and showed it with a frank grace which captivated the old soldier, as they stood together in the pleasant light of a mixed wood and coal fire, chatting about their young guest's journey and the festivity of to-morrow.

"Does Lou dine with us to-night?" asked the General.

"No," returned his wife; "Colonel Dalzell expects some friends from town."

"Then whom are we waiting for?"

"Oh! Lord Cecil Annesley. I met him to-day. He had just come over from Brittany, and stays for the dance. You know his brother commands the *Ariadne,* so I asked him to dinner."

"All right," returned Sir Frederic, "only I wish he would come. I am very hungry, and I am sure Miss Verner is 'famished.'"

"Lord Cecil Annesley," said a servant, throwing the door open in fulfilment of his master's wish.

"Very glad to see you!—dinner, Leonard, dinner at once," said the General in the same breath.

"Ah! that means I am late. A thousand apologies, my dear Lady Pearson; but just as I was leaving the hotel I was stopped by Frank Guthrie. You know Guthrie, the water-colour man?" etc. etc., and Lord Cecil rushed through a fluent apology. Lady Pearson assured him he was a very little behind time, and then introduced him to Miss Verner. Stasie, who was prepared to greet him cordially, was not a little chilled by his evident forgetfulness of her.

The announcement "Dinner is on table," however, cut short her slight embarrassment. She accepted Sir Frederic's offered arm, and went down to the dining-room.

Soup and fish had been served before Lord Cecil recognised the face and figure opposite him; then, in his surprise, he dropped his eye-glass as usual, and had a little difficulty in sticking it in its place again.

"Why, Miss Verner! Yes, of course I remember now. Had the pleasure of meeting you at Lady Elizabeth Wyatt's last season."

"I saw you did not know me at first," said Stasie, smiling, while a blush flitted across her cheek.

"I am infinitely flattered by your remembering *me*," he replied; "but the *rencontre* was so unexpected—I—I hope you will excuse me."

"Oh, yes, it was only natural. You see many more people than I do."

"But not many Miss Verners," said Sir Frederic gallantly.

"Ah! yes, to be sure. Mr. Wyatt is your guardian," remarked Lady Pearson. "Curious person Lady Elizabeth. she is always *entêté* on some subject; this season it was the education of women in Syria—elevating their position, and all that sort of thing. She always went about with that Eastern friend of yours, Miss Verner, and quite raved of him."

"What, of Hormuz Kharapet?" cried Stasie. "Well, he is very nice and clever; quite learned, indeed."

"He is in some way connected with you, is he not?" asked Lord Cecil. "Lady Elizabeth said something about it when I had the pleasure of meeting you."

"He is a sort of step-uncle, if there is such a relation," said Stasie, laughing. "He is my stepfather's brother."

"Hum! a connection, at any rate not within

the forbidden degree," returned Lord Cecil, significantly. Stasie understood him, and the telltale colour that came and went so readily flamed in her cheek for an instant, to Lady Pearson's alarm and disgust.

"It is amazing how women of condition can take up these fellows. I daresay Lady Elizabeth Wyatt would not let an Englishman of a corresponding grade farther than her servants' hall," observed the General.

"But, Sir Frederic, Mr. Kharapet is a gentleman," exclaimed Stasie. "His brother was our consul——"

"Really, my dear," cried Lady Pearson, "you ought not to speak so thoughtlessly. You forget his connection with this dear girl. You must not mind the General, Miss Verner; these old Indians have a most unreasoning contempt for every one of a different colour from themselves."

"But, do you know, Hormuz is fairer than Sir Frederic," said Stasie, gazing with simple honesty at the embrowned veteran, and quite innocent of intending to pay him back in his own coin.

The General perceived that she meant no

offence, and laughed good-humouredly—"Fairly
hit, Miss Verner. I must humbly beg pardon
for disparaging your *protégé.*"

"Why is it that you all look down on
Easterns? Mr. Kharapet is a Christian like
yourself," pursued Stasie, with some warmth.

"Like me? not a bit of it. I deny that *in
toto.*"

"Perhaps he is a better one," said Lord
Cecil.

"Very possibly; but still not like me," returned Sir Frederic. "Come, Miss Verner, take
a glass of wine with me in bygone fashion, as a
mark of forgiveness."

"Yes, certainly; but pray say no more against
Hormuz Kharapet. He has been very good to
me; *really* more obliging about things than Mr.
Harding."

"Ha! very likely. Deuced pretty little woman,
Mrs. Harding; I must confess to being deeply
smitten with Mrs. Harding," said Sir Frederic.

"And she is as nice as she is pretty," cried
Stasie, "and very, very clever."

"I imagine you are one of those lucky indi-
viduals whose friends are all highly and excep-

tionally gifted," observed Lord Cecil, as he helped himself to olives.

"Yes; I am lucky in believing them to be so at any rate, returned Stasie with some emphasis.

Lady Pearson laughed and nodded to her young friend, and then the conversation flowed away into other channels, till the hostess rose and led the way to the drawing-room.

"There is a beautiful moon," said Stasie, who had gone to the window to look out. "I am sure it will be fine to-morrow."

"Alas! in this climate we cannot be sure," replied Lady Pearson, who was reading some letters which had come by the last post; "but I think the weather promises to be fine."

"I do hope it will be, Lady Pearson. I quite long to dance again."

"I suppose you have not been to many dances, Miss Verner?"

"Pray call me 'Stasie,' Lady Pearson. I don't like the people I care for to call me 'Miss Verner.'"

"My dear child, that is very sweet of you. I shall always call you Stasie, for I feel as if you *were* my daughter. You know my only girl is married and so lost to me, I may say. However, I must not complain : she is very happy."

"Yes, it seems cruel," said Stasie thoughtfully ; "very cruel indeed, to lose a girl you have brought up and loved and cared for,—for eighteen or twenty years,—just because she fancies a stranger."

"It is, no doubt," replied Lady Pearson with a sentimental air. "Yet it is what all mothers wish for, to see their children—be they sons or daughters—happily settled—a mother's love is so unselfish. By the way, I am rather a foolish old woman about my children, and Van, your friend, is an especial pet : I must show you his last photograph." She rose and took from her work-table a morocco case, which she opened and handed to Stasie. It was a large full-length portrait in uniform, which was very becoming to the young lancer.

"How nice, how well he looks!" cried Stasie, in genuine hearty admiration. "I have never seen him in uniform ; I am sure it suits him."

"Remarkably well," said the gratified mother, coming to sit on the sofa beside her guest, and to gaze at the picture. "He looks most *dis-*

tingué in uniform, and indeed, though *I* say it, he is a son any parents might be proud of, so kind and warm-hearted, such a favourite in his regiment—a most promising officer—a little careless about money, but years will correct that."

"Oh, yes, it is ever so much better than being stingy. It must be delightful to have such a son. And he is very pleasant with us too ; we are always glad when he comes over, he is so bright and cheery," and Stasie continued to gaze with kindly admiration at the photograph. Lady Pearson's heart swelled with satisfaction ; surely her maternal schemes were certain of success.

"I suppose then, Stasie," she resumed, "you have not seen much of the gay world ?"

"Oh, dear no ! I have been at our school dances, of course, but yours was the only real ball I was ever at."

She did not add what disappointment and mortification it brought her.

"Was it, indeed ?" said Lady Pearson, anxious to get to the bottom of her intended daughter-in-law's present position and antecedents. "You must be rather dull, my poor child !"

"No, I don't think I am," returned Stasie a little uncertainly, and then glided gradually under Lady Pearson's judicious questioning into a full and confidential account of her life past and present, until the entrance of the gentlemen changed the subject.

The rest of the evening was passed by Lady Pearson and Lord Cecil in a game of picquet, and by Stasie in listening to some tiger hunting tales of Sir Frederic's, which, as they were heard for the first time really interested her, while her fingers were busy knitting a warm stocking destined for the use of Bhoodhoo during the cold days of coming winter.

Lord Cecil left early, and Stasie, somewhat tired with her journey and the excitement, went to bed.

So far everything surpassed her expectations. Lady Pearson was a dear, and as to the General, he was truly delightful. How nice, too, to see a mother so fond, and a son so deserving her fondness! How lucky she was to be noticed by such people! What a charming life they seemed to lead, so smooth, so animated! every one polite and well bred, with a pleasant word and suitable phrase ever at hand. What was it made the subtile charm of the evening ?

Then, as she brushed her long fair hair, she recalled the incidents of the day. The parting from Aunt Clem (she hoped that gentle spinster was not feeling very dull and low), finally, and with a shy reluctance even in thought, she lived through the few minutes she had spent with Dr. Brooke at the railway station.

He had been so nice the last two or three times they had met, only he was absurdly anxious about her health ! There was really nothing the matter with her, and she would not for worlds have Dr. Brooke prescribe for her, or feel her pulse, or look into her eyes with that searching glance of his. Heaven knows what secret weakness he might discover hidden away in the depths of her foolish heart. She wished he had left her a little bit of helwa ; she had got into the habit of eating a piece while going to bed. Why were good things always bad for one ! Then helwa led her thoughts to Bhoodhoo and to Kharapet. It was a shame of Sir Frederic to speak so slightingly of Kharapet—of any fellow-creature—yet she was conscious that his words did not wound her as they once would have done. She was curiously angry and disgusted with Kharapet. His avowals of love had had a strange effect ; she felt as if some hot sirocco had swept away the first freshness of her youth, and aged her before her time. Argue with herself as she would, repeat as she would that she was unjust, unkind, ungrateful (especially as he seemed now anxious to conform to her wishes), she could not away with the feeling that his love degraded her in her own eyes, that his touch was contamination !

Meantime Sir Frederic Pearson in the drawing-room below was enjoying the mingled comfort of a post-prandial glass of brandy and water, and a confidential talk with his wife.

"Do you know," said her ladyship, sipping a little soda and sherry, "I am quite convinced that dear girl is struck with Van ; a very little attention on his part will bring matters to a climax. If you had only seen the way she gazed at his photograph !"

"Pooh !" said the General. "Most girls like to look at a good-looking young fellow !"

"Yes, but she listened with such deep interest to all I said about him."

" Which I'll lay heavy odds was a good deal. We all know how long-winded you are when you begin talking about Van," returned the irreverent General.

" Well, my dear, have I not every right to be proud of him ?"

" Yes, yes, he is a fine fellow ; but don't you make too sure of the heiress. Why, there will be dozens after her, sharp men of the world who could buy and sell our boy !"

" She has seen but little as yet, and I am sure any girl might take a fancy to Van. I rather think he is really smitten with Stasie Verner !"

" Small blame to him ! She is a fine creature, an uncommon taking girl ; if she were to accept Van I should consider him a deuced lucky fellow."

" No doubt he would be most fortunate, so pray, my dear, be guided by me. The sooner we can make sure of her the better, both for her and ourselves, pray do not ask any of those young dandies of the Rifles, or that beauty man—what's his name—of the Marine Artillery !"

Sir Frederic laughed a loud jolly laugh.

" Why, after all, I think more of the boy than

you do! I think he is a match for those men in every way."

"I am sure *I* think so, but then there is no accounting for a girl's whims."

"Ah, ha! then you are *not* quite so sure of her, my lady! Quite right; never count your chickens——"

"Really, Sir Frederic," interrupted his wife, "those old sayings are very stupid!"

.   .   .   .   .

For once the weather was lenient to the projected dance.

Stasie woke to see a bright blaze of morning light shimmering over the sea, which laughed back again in a thousand ripples, as though life were one prolonged morning-tide of youth and joy.

Stasie peeped delighted through her Venetian blinds at this inspiriting outlook. She felt unusually well, with something of that delicious sense of vivid life in her heart and veins, which used to make bare existence a delight. Lately she had been a stranger to this sensation, but probably change of air and a slight degree of fatigue had ensured her an unusually good night. Certainly she felt wonderfully better and brighter than she did the day before. No doubt change *was* what she wanted, and she would return to Sefton Park strengthened, refreshed, and quite superior to Dr. Brooke's pitying, inquiring glances.

She was completely dressed for some time before the breakfast bell rang, and busied herself writing part at least of a letter to Mrs. Harding, to be finished after her return from the dance. She had despatched a hasty line to Aunt Clem before dinner the previous day.

Stasie was greeted with the most affectionate inquiries as to how she had slept, and whether she had been comfortable, etc. etc. She found Lady Pearson sitting behind a big tea-urn, in a becoming morning gown and lace-edged muslin cap, while the embrowned stately General looked fresh and well in a rough gray suit, with snowy linen and a coloured tie.

He was kindly and attentive to his wife as well as to his guest, giving them morsels of news from the *Times*, at which he glanced occasionally, and rising with cheerful alacrity to obey his wife's orders when she desired him to bring the preserves or to cut her some of the cold beef which was upon the sideboard. Stasie thought that if men were all like Sir Frederic, one or two would be rather an improvement to most homes, a matter she had sometimes doubted when in Mr. Harding's.

"I think you were a true prophet, my dear," said Lady Pearson, as she handed Stasie her tea. "We shall have a lovely day I hope. What time does the eight o'clock train from Waterloo reach Portsmouth, General? Van was to try and catch it."

"It's a slow train—devilish slow parliamentary affair!—does not get in till eleven or eleven-thirty, I think."

"I hope Mr. Pearson will come," cried Stasie. "I shall be so utterly strange if he does not, and he dances so well."

"I think you may be pretty sure of him," said his mother with a pleased smile. "He certainly is a good partner."

"By George! you'll have no lack of partners, I'll be bound," cried the gallant General.

"Still, I should like Mr. Pearson to come," added Stasie.

Lady Pearson meanwhile had opened some of her letters. "Frank says they are going to have

a grand football match with the Hadleigh Club
on the thirteenth ; he thinks his side sure to win.
I wish there was no such game ; it is most dangerous and brutal," she said, looking to her husband.

"Pooh ! nonsense !" he returned. "It is no
worse than other games. English boys do not
care for play that [has not a spice of danger
in it."

"Football is much worse than anything else,"
persisted Lady Pearson. "Frank is our youngest
boy," she explained to Stasie. "He is going to
try for the Civil Service, and is now staying with
some friends in Yorkshire for a little relaxation.
He has been working very hard."

The General made a grimace that provoked
Stasie to laughter.

"You are too bad, Fred," cried his wife.
"Well, Stasie, what should you like to do this
morning? You must keep rather quiet on account of the dance. We must take good care of
you, and send you back quite strong and well to
your aunt."

"Oh ! Lady Pearson, I don't care what we do.
I should like to go out on the beach, but I shall

be quite content to sit in the window with a book ; this is such a delicious, lovely place."

"If you don't want to go very early to the club, General, you might take Stasie for a stroll on the beach."

"I am quite at Miss Verner's service, if she will allow me to finish the *Times*."

"Oh, of course ! I am so much obliged, Sir Frederic ; I am afraid it will bore you."

"What a cross-grained old hunks you must think me ! I consider it an honour to be your escort. There—I don't think Van could say anything better, eh ! Miss Verner ?"

"No, certainly not ! *No* one could ; only please don't call me Miss Verner."

"Come then, you will find the piano and some magazines in the drawing-room," said Lady Pearson ; "and just do as you like, dear, until the General is ready. I must answer some of these letters."

But Stasie felt rather shy of playing or singing among strangers, so she took *Temple Bar* and sat down in the window.

But the sunshine and movement outside were too much for the attractions of even Miss Brad-

don's most thrilling tales, and the distant sound
of military music filled her with a vague pleasure.
She sat in a kind of dream, from which she was
roused by a sweet but rather high pitched voice
saying—

"Miss Verner, let me introduce myself, as I
cannot find my mother. Mrs. Dalzell, Miss
Verner—Miss Verner, Mrs. Dalzell. Now we are
en règle, I suppose you know who I am?"

"Oh, yes! quite well," cried Stasie, who had
started up, and shook hands with a slight elegant-
looking little brunette, in a sort of yachting costume. She was a diminished, softened, beauti-
fied likeness of the General, but with a restless
expression very different from his.

" So you are Miss Verner," she resumed, throwing herself into an easy-chair. " I want to look
at you and consider you, for I have heard a good
deal of you, and of course you are not a bit like
what I expected. They said you were fair, and
I cannot bear blondes; they generally want salt,
but your eyes redeem you! Am I impertinent?
I have the credit of it, but I am only frank.
Ah! you do not like to be stared at."

" I do not think any one does," said Stasie

with some spirit, "but at least I can look at you in return."

"Good!" cried the little lady, clapping her hands. "Am *I* like what you expected?"

"I had no expectations," replied Stasie candidly.

Mrs. Dalzell laughed merrily. "That is flattering; pray did Van—did my brother never mention me to you?"

"Oh, yes! but not often."

"Good-for-nothing boy! and I gave him the sweetest little dog, which I believe he passed on to you."

"Was Pearl yours? He is a dear little creature."

Having thus cleared all formalities at a bound, Mrs. Dalzell proceeded to ingratiate herself with Stasie by a series of compliments disguised as fault-finding, and finally proposed going out, pooh-poohing the projected escort of Sir Frederic.

"Papa would much rather sit indoors and read the *Times* from the births, deaths, and marriages to 'vivat regina,' and I shall amuse you much more. I want some flowers and some silks. I am a great lover of fancy-work, are you ?"

" No. I rather like common useful work. I am not clever enough to do pretty things."

" You do not give me that idea. By the way, how frightfully dull you must be at that place— what do you call it—something Park. How do you manage to live ?"

" It is not so bad," replied Stasie, who was not accustomed to look on existence as a mere play-ground, and thereupon Mrs. Dalzell led her young companion into a long and full description of her home and surroundings. She manipulated her subject much more skilfully than her mother did, and drew rather different conclusions.

.   .   .   .   .

When Stasie and her new acquaintance returned from their ramble they found the house in some excitement. Mr. Pearson had arrived rather earlier than was expected, had breakfasted and made his toilette, and came beaming out of the dining-room to meet them. Stasie was delighted to see him. He was like an old friend in that strange place.

" Oh ! I am so glad you have come," cried

Stasie, with sparkling eyes and sweetest smile, " I was afraid something might have prevented you."

" It must have been a strong reason that would have kept me away," he returned with much significance. " And we are going to have such a jolly day! One is always on the stretch in this climate until you know what the weather is to be. Why, Miss Verner, you look pounds better already! Do you know, Lou, she is just bored to death at Sefton Park! *You* would commit suicide after ten days of it, and the victim is not even aware of her martyrdom."

" She is not indeed," said Stasie, laughing, as they went up to the drawing-room, where was a lovely bouquet, fresh from Covent Garden, in its newly-opened box, an offering from the enamoured lancer to the heiress.

She was enchanted, but not intoxicated. In the course of conversation young Pearson said, " I fell in with your friend Mr. Harding yesterday morning in the city. Wonderful thing for me to visit that money-making centre. He is going away somewhere."

" Is he? That is quite unexpected."

" I daresay his wife will not be inconsolable, and at any rate she has that tall relative to look after her, which I have no doubt he will. Brooke can be a very pleasant fellow if he likes."

The words seemed to lay an icy grasp on Stasie's heart for a moment ; the sunshine was no longer joyous but cruelly fierce ; the pleasant sound of cheerful voices was a confusing murmur ; the scent of the flowers was heavy and sickening. Was it possible that others beside Aunt Clem and herself noticed Brooke's devotion to his cousin ? And if there was reason for such remarks, why was she so strongly moved by them ? The only sufferer from such a state of feeling would be Brooke himself ; and of course she was sorry for him. He had been kind and interested in her. She would banish these uncomfortable thoughts. Why should Dr. Brooke, or the ideas he suggested, come to tarnish the vivid brightness of her rare pleasure as he did once before ? She had been silent but a moment and what a tide of thought and conjecture had swept over her brain ! As she looked up to answer some question of Lady Pearson's, she met Mrs. Dalzell's keen eyes fixed on her with startling intensity.

It was unpleasant for the instant, but the impression soon passed away.

.   .   .   .   .

The dance was most successful. To Stasie it was a scene of enchantment, from the start in the steam-launch to the return at sundown, when the young moon began to throw a shimmer of silver over the sea.

The quarterdeck was converted into a huge tent, embanked with greenery and beautiful flowers ; the band inspiriting ; the boards perfection ; partners flocked in files to be presented to the fair girl whose fortune suffered no diminution by report.

She gave an open preference, however, to her original cavalier, and a general conviction that Van Pearson was a " deuced lucky fellow " was adopted in both services.

That young gentleman was not so elate as might have been expected. He had the instinct of an honest heart, and was not inordinately conceited, considering his years and profession. His mind misgave him that the liking so frankly shown was not exactly like a young girl's manifestation of love; still it was all very pleasant and encouraging.

The days that followed were diversified by visits to Cowes, to Carisbrooke, to the *Victory* (of course), and sundry other legitimate points of attraction.

Mrs. Dalzell's untiring thirst for pleasure, her wilfulness and playful tyranny over her grim-looking husband, once a *beau sabreur*, amused Stasie immensely. She did not feel inclined to trust her, yet could not help liking her. " Van " got a few days' leave, and did his best to improve the shining hour, but was less prompt in his action than his mother wished.

" Really, my dear boy, I do not know how much more encouragement you want," said Lady Pearson, as she sat in conclave with her son and daughter after luncheon one afternoon, when Stasie had been about ten days their guest. " What *is* the use of losing time ? If Stasie Verner is unmarried, and goes out with Lady Elizabeth Wyatt next season, your chances will be considerably diminished. Why, even now that stupid Lord Cecil is not without his pretensions. You will lose her if you don't take care."

" And I can tell you, mother, I shall lose her if

I am too prompt. She is not one bit in love with me ! and I fancy I haven't as good a chance here, as in that infernal hole, where I am the only bit of life she sees."

" I imagine Van is right, mother ! " said Mrs. Dalzell thoughtfully. " I do not quite understand Stasie Verner. What sort of man is this Brooke of whom I have heard you speak ? "

" A tall, grave, sombre fellow, not at all handsome. Looks like a gentleman, though. I believe he did some very gallant things attending to the wounded under fire in India, but, oh ! there is no danger there ! He takes very little notice of Miss Verner. I see that Kharapet and Miss Stretton think he is sweet on Mrs. Harding— can't see it myself."

" Well, I have pressed Stasie to give us another week. She has just gone to write to her aunt about it. You might get leave for a day or two more, and then——"

Further projects and plans were cut short by the entrance of the Pearsons' servant bearing a coloured envelope on a salver. Lady Pearson opened, glanced at it, gave a slight scream, and lay back in her chair. Her son seized and read it aloud.

"Frank had a bad accident yesterday—come to him at once."

"The football match," cried Mrs. Dalzell, turning pale.

CHAPTER II.

WHEN Brooke had seen the train disappear which carried Stasie away, as he fondly hoped, to fresh air and renewed strength, he turned to Miss Stretton, and asked if he could do anything for her, or stay with her till the next train to Sefton Park.

"Many thanks, my dear sir! I will not put your politeness to so severe a proof; as I *am* in town, I will take the opportunity to do a little shopping. I can go to Waterloo House, at least, and catch the six o'clock down train. Ah, how lost I shall feel in choosing even the most insignificant article without that dear child."

"No doubt," said Brooke sympathetically.

"So if you would be good enough to call a cab I shall trouble you no further."

Brooke complied with her request, and then descending the steps on the arrival side of the station, walked slowly on towards West-minster.

Passing along York Road his eye was caught by some flaming placards of a sensational drama, then enjoying the glories of a prolonged run.

The interest of the piece centered round a mysterious case of poisoning, and reminded Brooke of the intention with which he had taken Stasie's sweeties from her. He drew the neat parcel of Helwa from his pocket, and, taking out a gray morsel, proceeded to eat it as he went along. The sight of that flaring poster had set him thinking deeply and uneasily. He had seen Stasie set out on her journey with a mixture of satisfaction and anxiety. That she would be clear of Sefton Park, Kharapet, and that doubtful Indian servant for a fortnight or three weeks, was an infinite relief. It gave him breathing time; it freed him from the terrible blinding fear of what each day, each hour, might bring forth, which robbed him of his cooler judgment—of the power of weighing evidence, of coming to any-thing like a clearly reasoned-out conclusion.

Now for a short time his fears were at rest. He could examine the circumstances of the case,

the sources of the horrible doubt which assailed
him.   Even a cursory glance at the dark array
of details which awaited his careful consideration,
showed him the enormous difficulties with which
he would have to contend should he on more
mature reflection still think Stasie's life in
danger.   Good God! What an awful thought!
and her bright face, full of anticipated pleasure,
yet remembering Aunt Clem's feelings even in
her own joy, rose before him.   Nevertheless
this same visit from which he hoped so much
might destroy all chance of his own success.
No doubt Lady Pearson would throw her as
much as possible with her son, and what more
natural than that the *debonnair* young soldier
should be acceptable to an inexperienced girl
new to the world, and ready to gild most
things by the light of her own imagination;
but even as the strong probability of such an
ending came before him Brooke felt that his
own disappointment would bring with it a
degree of comfort.   Young Pearson, though
much below Stasie's moral and intellectual stan-
dard, was, Brooke believed, a good, honest fellow, and with him her sweet young life would

be safe. How bitter a disappointment such an untying of the present hard knot would be none but himself could know. Stasie was seldom out of his thoughts, not only on account of the strange fears he entertained for her, but because of the remarkable way in which she seemed to have closed the petals of her soul against him.

During the first weeks of their acquaintance he had been half amused, half flattered by the eager pleasure with which she sought his society and conversation, although he was clear-sighted enough to perceive there was not a tinge of coquetry or ordinary love of admiration in her innocent preference. But from the hour he stupidly misunderstood her, and no doubt showed his misunderstanding, she changed to him, in a subtile secret way that none save he himself could perceive, and from that time, too, he became aware that she was more to him than any other woman ever had been before. Now, she had indeed become "the ocean to the river of his thoughts." Was it possible that any man breathed so cruel, so vile, as to plot against the life of this fair, noble, generous-hearted creature?

"Dr. Brooke, you are in such deep thought

you walk against me." Looking up with a start, Brooke found himself face to face with Kharapet at the corner of Parliament Street.

"I beg your pardon," he exclaimed with an odd dazed feeling as if some evil omen had suddenly blighted him. "I was, as you say, lost in thought."

"It is a lovely day," said Kharapet, lingering as if he did not know exactly how to break off once he had begun to talk. "I am sure the English climate is much belied, and I am hastening to enjoy the fine evening with my friends at Sefton Park."

"You will probably meet Miss Stretton; there is no train before six thirty, and she returns by it."

"Returns," echoed Kharapet devouring his interlocutor for a moment with big hungry eyes, as if greatly surprised. "Has Miss Stretton been in town to-day?"

"She has, I have just left her. We were starting Miss Verner off for Southsea."

Kharapet had sufficient self-control to fix his eyes on the ground, yet he could not quite hide the change which passed over his face.

"Stasie gone to Southsea! how—how is this? I was not informed—I—I——" he stopped abruptly. Brooke watched the Syrian's uneasiness and confusion, not without a degree of pleasure; he was thoroughly roused, every faculty keenly alive.

"Young Pearson came over yesterday with a note from his mother," replied Brooke carelessly. "It seems there is an afternoon dance, or a kick-up of some description, to-morrow, and Lady Pearson wished Miss Verner to assist, in the French sense. Miss Stretton hesitated, but we all backed up Miss Verner, who was of course wild to go; and she is gone."

Kharapet was silent for a few minutes, and then said with a harsh laugh, "You were certainly prompt. The one thing in English life I neither understand nor approve is your neglect of your young ladies. I had intended escorting Stasie to Southsea myself. It is not well on Miss Stretton's part to let her go alone."

A scornful reply rose to Brooke's lips, but he restrained it. It would not do to defy Kharapet in any case. If the deep-dyed scoundrel Brooke suspected, he was a power not to be trifled with, and must be fought with his own weapons. If innocent, why, he was harmless, and deserved decent treatment.

"Well, you see ideas on these matters differ! You are on your way to the Hardings? Pray tell Mrs. Harding I shall not be down for two or three days."

The Syrian promised politely to deliver the message, and they parted, going opposite ways.

"That fellow will be down on Aunt Clem," said Brooke to himself. "He is awfully cut up at Stasie's taking the law into her own hands! Is it possible that such a quiet, mild kind of man could conspire against the life of a fellow-creature, and such a creature? but the look he gave her that day was deadly. Pooh! I must not let imagination run away with me. I'll eat every scrap of this sweet stuff before I come to any conclusion. The last certainly did me no harm, and if this too is harmless, why, that will score one to Kharapet. It must be deucedly difficult to poison *one* member of a family."

So musing, he proceeded to transact some business at Grindlay's, where he met an acquaintance who was passing through town, and with whom he dined at the club.

· · · · ·

A few evenings after Brooke returned early to his lodgings, intending to work for an hour or two on a paper which he was preparing for a medical journal. The occupation was a relief. It drew him from the subject on which he dwelt so continuously and so painfully. He spread out his notes, which he consulted from time to time, and wrote steadily for an hour or two.

The servant of the house brought him a caraffe of cold water with a tumbler, as was her custom, before asking formally if he "wanted anything more." On the tray was a note from Mrs. Harding asking him to perform some trifling commission, and adding "You will be glad to hear that Stasie Verner is enjoying herself immensely, and says she feels wonderfully better—quite herself again. I fancy her fortnight will stretch into three weeks. Mr. Pearson rode over yesterday, and says she made quite a sensation at the *Ariadne* dance. He goes down again to-morrow, at which I am *not* pleased. When am I to see you again?"

Brooke pulled his moustaches gravely as he perused this epistle. What a trump Livy was, and how little he had remembered her or her troubles of late! His conscience smote him. After a pause he folded up the note and applied himself to his work, but had hardly written for a quarter of an hour when he suddenly dropped his pen, and, seizing the arms of his chair, sat rigid and still, while his breath came quickly. He had been struck by a sensation of increased warmth which for some minutes had been spreading over his body, and now his heart beat wildly, as if it would burst its bounds. The sideboard opposite him, the mantelpiece and its ornaments, seemed slowly turning round, and a feeling of nausea oppressed him! "I know what wine I have taken to-day," he murmured to himself, "and this cannot be intoxication." He rose to his feet, and by a strong effort steadied himself to cross the room, and throw open the window in order to get air. Leaning out, he observed that foot-passengers and vehicles seemed to move in an odd, wavering, impossible manner. Slightly revived, he struggled to the fireplace, and looked, with a half-articulate exclamation of horror, at the reflection of his eyes in the glass, at the dilated pupils, the wild staring look. It was the same, only exaggerated, which had alarmed him in Stasie's and especially roused his suspicions.

Throwing himself into a chair, he buried his face in his hands, and remained a few minutes in deep thought. Then he again started to his feet, and, staggering to the sideboard, took out some brandy and swallowed a glass. He stood still, his hand resting on the back of a chair, until he began to feel more himself. His heart ceased to beat in heavy thumps, his vision grew clearer. At last, with a deep sigh of relief, he again approached the window, and drew a long breath.

"I have it now," he thought. "I have at length swallowed some portion of the helwa more saturated with the poison than the rest. Yesterday I was slightly affected, so slightly that but for *this* experience I should not have remembered it. It cannot yet be two hours since I ate the last piece! The infernal villains! they are using some alkaloid poison. Nothing else can account for Stasie's symptoms or my own. It is a devilish plot. I know how almost impossible it is to detect. The symptoms, too, can be so easily

attributed to heart disease or other natural disorders ; and more, the doses may be so regulated
as to cause a gradual decay of strength ! how can
I act, or rather counteract ? "

At this point of his reflections Brooke ceased
to think clearly or consecutively. A whirling
cloud of terrible apprehension and of self-
distrust of painful anticipation seemed to enfold
his brain, and take from him the power of con-
trolling its action.

The cold sweat stood in big beads upon his
brow, and his strong frame quivered with a
nameless fear.

" What could he do ? Gradually he recovered, and by an enormous effort of will, compelled himself to examine the position critically
and coolly.

First, he felt sure that Kharapet had determined to remove the obstacle which stood
between him and fortune, the girl whose rejection had swept away the slender barrier that
divides such passion as he could feel, from hatred
and vengeance. For this he had introduced the
Hindoo servant into Stasie's establishment, and
with a view to the probable termination of his

attempt, he had told Dr. Hunter that Stasie's mother had died of heart disease.

Kharapet's position gave him great advantages ; he evidently had some occult influence over Mr. Harding, he was a special favourite with Mr. Wyatt, he was the *deus ex machina* for good to Stasie's aunt. He was a man of irreproachable character ; he stood well with irreproachable and influential people. It would be dangerous to attack him, for attack would only serve to strengthen him by its failure. What proof could Brooke offer that this paragon was carrying out a diabolical plot against the life of an unoffending girl? The tendency of the British mind would be to pooh - pooh such dramatic transpontine villainy at once. Such goings on within the sacred circle of whited sepulchres, were incredible, impossible ! Reason, common-sense, self-interest forbid them. " Is it likely a man already making his way successfully would run the awful, imminent risk of discovery, of ruin, of life, for a comparatively small stake ? *no* game could be worth such a candle ! " Brooke imagined the average Englishman saying. But if it were next to impossible that detection could overtake him, the Syrian *would* dare to destroy! At that time alkaloid poisons were very little known in England; moreover, Brooke reflected that much of the untamed savage still lurked under the thin lacquer of European civilisation.

What was he to do? He ran over in his mind the people by whom Stasie was surrounded. The Hardings? it would be simple folly to name the subject to them. Miss Stretton? she was so bewitched by Kharapet that if she saw him administering certified poison, she would not believe it. Little Robinson might perhaps on good proof credit him with sharp practice in money matters, but nothing more. Dr. Hunter? pooh, an old woman! No; he was single-handed against desperate odds! And Stasie herself? At the thought of her his heart swelled with tenderness and compassion, with intense longing; to her of all others, he dared not breathe his terrible fears; she would laugh him to scorn; yet he must, he would save her.

Then Brooke strove to picture to himself Kharapet's probable line of action. He would not do what he had set himself to do quickly.

No, the wretch had nearly three years before him, unless, indeed, Stasie married. He could weaken her, produce repeated attacks, apparently of heart disease or softening of the brain ; and then whenever a necessity arose, if she were about to be married, or approaching her majority, he could kill with one dose, the traces of which would, more than probably, evaporate before an examination could be made. What a crowd of hideous images thronged Brooke's mind as this idea presented itself !

Look at circumstances which way he would, he saw but one way of escape. Stasie must marry as soon as possible, but whom ? himself ? If—*if* only he could win her, all might go well ; for danger, though round her, was not imminent. Ah ! what a delicious remedy, could he but persuade her to adopt it,—if !

Four months ago, he should not have so doubted his own powers ; but now, suppose she rejected him ? he would lose his power to help her, or weaken it fatally. He must proceed with the utmost caution, with profoundest watchfulness. If Kharapet perceived that he sought Stasie, that he aspired to wed her, and was likely to succeed, it might be her death warrant! and if he seemed to make love to her *sub rosa*, it might rouse her high spirit.   Come what may, however, he would do his best to win her, and why should he not succeed?   New life seemed to thrill through his veins as he contemplated this possibility ; his pulses throbbed with fresh vigour.   The only chance for his love, his Hebe, his beautiful Stasie, lay in their making what is called making a bolt of it!   Disreputable but delicious alternative !

Now, to review the forces on his side—first his own energy and quick sight, sharpened by intense feeling ; next Mrs. Harding, she would help him in all ways with Stasie, and be as useful as an ally could be, whose eyes were but half open ; lastly Sir Harcourt Filmer, the leading authority on heart disorders.   He was Brooke's former master and present friend, a man of great attainments, of liberal and extended views.   *He* might be trusted and might afford valuable help, to him alone could Brooke confide his discovery, his fears."

And that cursed helwa ! there was still a lot of it.   He was not inclined to repeat the dose just then, but he would eat some each day, carefully noticing the effects. He was sure the poison was unequally distributed in the sweetmeat, probably by design.

Even so much determined on was a relief, though Brooke sat on and on, far into the night, reviewing his extraordinary position from every point of view.

If—if only Filmer would take up his views, he might suggest some line of conduct more efficient than any which had yet occurred to himself.

. . . . .

"DEAR ROBINSON—Do you never give yourself a holiday? I have hitherto always been your guest. Can you manage to come with me up the river? We used both to pull a pretty good oar at one time. We'll get away by train to Richmond, have our spurt, and dine together after. I am rather out of sorts, and have prescribed for myself a course of social enjoyment, which you must help me to carry out, as I will explain. Get the curate at Welwood to take your morning prayers, and I'll put you up. I will take no excuse, though you may take your own time.—Yours always, J. BROOKE."

This note reached the Rev. St. John Robinson the evening after Brooke had the attack above described.

The young divine was enjoying a cup of tea after a hard day's work, for it was that on which he was in the habit of assisting his friend the curate with a distant parish, also held by the Rector of Sefton.

It was a tempting invitation.

Robinson's holidays were few and far between ; and for reasons best known to himself he did not that autumn choose to take his usual three weeks' leave of absence.

Neither life nor work were exhilarating at Sefton Park. To a high-toned spiritually-minded young minister there is probably nothing more discouraging than the snug self-content of the ordinary well-to-do irreproachable citizen, whose life affords no excuse for meddling to the ardent ecclesiastic. The Rev. St. John felt that a day or two with his friend would be an immense refreshment. His old schoolboy liking for Brooke had revived and deepened ; their dissimilarity of thought and opinion gave charm and variety to their talk, and after an hour or two passed with his friend, Robinson generally felt a new man.

He at once set about making the necessary arrangements, and early in the ensuing week the friends met to carry out Brooke's programme.

The weather, however, was not propitious; it was dull and oppressive, and though unmistakably glad to see him, Brooke appeared unusually preoccupied. He looked worn too; his deep eyes had a restless expression, his thin temples seemed more craggy than usual. After a while he grew more like himself, and talked with less effort.

The rowing was something of a failure—both were out of practice, and a slow drizzle induced them to return to the hotel, where they had ordered dinner, sooner than they intended; and having reached it, the rain, which had driven them in, ceased; the low dun gray clouds, slowly parting, drifted eastward as a breeze sprang up and revealed the glories of a fine sunset.

Brooke and his friend strolled slowly to and fro the terrace before the hotel, enjoying the view, and gradually growing more and more confidential in their talk.

" You are looking rather seedy," said Brooke,

as he lit a cigar and offered his case to Robinson. "Why don't you take a run over to Switzerland or Brittany? The most complete change is somewhere away on the Continent."

"I don't care to go this year," with a slight sigh; "I prefer sticking to my work—and, Brooke, you are looking out of sorts yourself."

"I know I am," returned Brooke grimly. "Tell me about yourself, Robby." (This had been the Reverend St. John's school appellation.)

"There isn't much to tell. I am singularly well placed in some respects. The freedom, the position, an incumbency gives is, of course, a great advantage; but the income is as yet small and a little uncertain; in fact, barely enough for a bachelor."

"A bachelor, eh! Then you are thinking of becoming a benedict?"

"No, Brooke; not thinking of it. Perhaps were I quite sure it is desirable for a priest to marry, I might wish to do so."

"Don't call yourself a priest, Robby; it is a term I am not fond of. Well, and why should it not be desirable for a clergyman to marry?"

"There is much to be said for and against,"

returned Robinson thoughtfully. "I am by no means in favour of compulsory celibacy; but the ideal priest (you must let me use the word, it conveys to my mind a clear impression) should stand above these mere earthly ties ; no human love ought to come between him and the spiritual life, of which he should be an example, and yet ——" the young man sighed.

"He would be a deuced deal better priest if he were an honest citizen, with family ties like his neighbours," put in Brooke very decidedly.

" And yet a home—and there is no such thing without a woman to make it—must be sweet, very sweet," resumed Robinson ; " and to many marriage is a safe refuge; still, the ideal man of God, strong and tender, absolved from the dominion of self-love, and caring for wandering sinners, bringing them home to their Father's fold, himself purified from earthly passion, is a glorious figure."

"Not to my mind. I prefer the full exercise of all the faculties bestowed on us. Why, you rob yourself of part of your rightful inheritance in resisting the strongest instinct of our nature ; the result of such fruitless self-mastery will be 'wisdom from one entrance quite shut out.'"

"Do you not yourself wilfully shut out one class of wisdom, and of a very high class, Brooke?"

"Not wilfully. But come, I'll read your riddle: you are in love, Robby."

That reverend gentleman blushed, but shook his head. "No," he said, "not in love. I think I am sufficiently lord of myself to regulate my feelings; yet were I sure, were it clear to me, that marriage would not militate against the usefulness of my office, I might—that is, I know a young lady who would make an admirable helpmeet."

"Is she at Sefton Park?" asked Brooke drily.

"She is," returned the young incumbent, who, having broken the ice, was once more at ease.

Can it be that he has fallen in love with Stasie Verner? thought Brooke. I hope not; he might as well cry for the moon. "Do I know the lady?"

"Yes, I think you have met her; she was at the school-feast, and is often with Mrs. Harding."

"Not Miss Verner?"

"Oh dear, no. Miss Verner is quite absorbed

by Mr. Pearson. But have you not met a slight girl with dark brown hair, and dark eyes, and a remarkably sweet smile ? If you have, you could not fail to observe her."

" You are evidently far gone, Robby," said his friend with a good-natured smile. " Who is the young lady ? "

" A Miss Morison—Miss Marion Morison—they, I mean the family, live opposite me at Sefton Park."

" What ? the people who flatten their noses against the window panes to peep at you ? "

" Only the younger ones ! not Marion. She is quite above such things," cried Robinson, and proceeded with some eagerness to dilate on the position and prospects of his lady love, the eldest daughter of a gentleman who was at the head of a large business.

While he talked Brooke's thoughts flew back to the objects seldom absent from them. How curious this surface crust of ordinary every-day life, with its humble hopes and ambitions; its small loves and dislikes and efforts, lightly skinning over the hot lava of deadly hatred—cruelty, crime, which rolled its heated tide below ! Could his terrible suspicions be true? At times he doubted their possibility; again he was firmly convinced of their reality; and though for a blessed week or two he was at rest (no harm could come to Stasie while under Sir Frederic Pearson's roof), but he dreaded the coming time when she would be helpless in the hands of her executioner. Dreaming over it, however, could do no good. He must plan to be near her, to carry out as quickly as possible the only way of rescue which at present suggested itself. He must keep his head cool, his nerves steady, or he could be of no use.

Here a waiter informed the gentlemen that their dinner was ready, and so cut short the stream of Robinson's eloquence. There is always a pleasing diversion in dinner; and with all his spiritual and lover-like aspirations the amiable incumbent felt its cheering effect.

"Take another glass of claret, Robinson," said Brooke, after the cheese had been removed. "It is better than I expected. I feel considerably the better, too, of our expedition, though it might have been more successful. London at this season is not inspiriting."

"Why don't you go away somewhere? You can do as you like."

"Yes, but I want to stay in London or its neighbourhood. You see I have to make up my mind between this and the end of January whether I shall return to India or not, and I want to study my ground. My old friend Filmer will be in town again in about ten days or so, and I look for sound advice from him."

"Don't go back to India, Brooke. I am sure you would do well in London."

"I don't know, but at present it is not a cheerful residence. Now you have a large house. Suppose you let me chum with you? I don't think we should bore each other?"

"Chum?" repeated Robinson with a note of interrogation.

"Yes, it is our word in India for sharing house and housekeeping with another fellow. Let me come and live with you, you have plenty of room."

"I am sure I should be very glad—only, you see," growing a little red, "I have no furniture in the rooms."

"No matter; with us the other fellow always brings his own sticks."

"If you really care to come," cried Robinson in his natural cheery, kindly voice, "that would simplify matters, and *I* should be delighted. But to be perfectly candid, I am not quite sure how Mrs. Harris would take it. You see she is a most respectable person, and quite invaluable to me, as my aunt said, but a little peculiar in temper."

"So I imagine. But Robby, we must reconcile her to my awful presence. What's to be done?"

"I do not exactly know, but I think she rather likes you. She said one morning, as she was clearing away breakfast, that you were not the ordinary run of whipper-snappers!"

"I am an extraordinary whipper-snapper then!" said Brooke, laughing. "Well, try and make terms with your ruler; tell her I am the most inoffensive chap breathing, easily pleased, content with a dietary of chops and rice pudding, and willing not only to brush my own boots but to give hers a polish at the same time. See if you can't manage this for me, Robby? and as soon as you can."

Robinson looked at him, a good deal puzzled

by his eagerness. "I am afraid you will be bored in my quiet abode, but for me it will be uncommonly jolly to have you ——"

"Just fancy what it is to be alone in London lodgings at this season, and you will understand what a change for the better it will be to chum with you," returned Brooke.

"Why, we shall be quite a cheery party at Sefton Park in a week or two," said Robinson, rubbing his hands. "The Hardings stay till near Christmas, Miss Verner will return about the 30th; Kharapet, whom I met yesterday, tells me he is coming down to stay at Limeville as soon as she is at home, so with the addition of yourself ——"

"I suppose," interrupted Brooke, "that impulsive young spinster Miss Stretton does not think it proper to entertain so fascinating a youth as Kharapet in her niece's absence!"

Robinson laughed. "Don't be cynical, Brooke! There cannot be a better woman than Miss Stretton; and as to Kharapet, do you know, he is really a good fellow. He takes quite an interest in my permanent church fund. He has subscribed ten pounds himself, and collected fifteen more among his friends ; and let me tell you, twenty-five pounds is no contemptible sum when the subscription goes on so slowly. Ah ! a real stone church would have a most beneficial effect, not only on the worshippers but on my position."

"Then I drink to its success. But I wish you had none of that Syrian devil's money in your bag."

"Really, Brooke, you are too prejudiced. The more I know him the more I like him."

Brooke growled something inarticulate, and then asked "if there were any tidings of Miss Verner ?"

"Yes ; I heard from Mrs. Harding that she was wonderfully better, and enjoying herself immensely—dances and excursions, and all sorts of amusements. Young Pearson is always there 'making hay while the sun shines, I suppose.'"

"I suppose so," said Brooke, and straightway fell into deep thought, saying little more till they reached town, Mr. Robinson being so deeply interested in his own hopes, fears, and doubts that he scarce noticed his companion's silence.

" Be sure you open the trenches with Mrs. Harris at once," were Brooke's last words. " I want to take up my residence with you as soon as possible."

CHAPTER III.

"THAT little beggar Robinson is going it, *I* can tell you," said Mr. Harding to his wife, as he sipped a glass of port after dinner. "Why, there was half a ship's cargo with his name on the packages down at the station."

"Indeed! I have not seen him for a few days. I suppose he has been extra busy?"

"I should think so! I met him going down to the station to look after his goods and chattels, and he tells me he is furnishing a bedroom for Brooke—your cousin, the doctor—who is going to put up with him for a bit."

"Is he?" said Mrs. Harding, suppressing any expression of the surprise she felt. "I wonder he cares to come to this place. It cannot be very attractive."

"Hum! that shows all you know about it," with a sneer. "There's attraction enough here,

I suspect, though the doctor is a cool customer, and doesn't show his hand. I'll be curious to see Kharapet's face when he comes down and finds him settled here! Kharapet's conceit is too much for any man to stomach since he has been staying with those blank, blank psalm-singing nobs! What can you expect when a sneaking native finds himself petted up by English lords and ladies? By George! it's enough to make a dog sick. But I suspect he has met his match in our young friend —— me! but she is a trump."

"There is certainly very little chance for Mr. Kharapet with Stasie," remarked Mrs. Harding, lifting her eyes from a book she was reading.

Mr. Harding growled something inarticulate, and seemed thoughtful for a moment. "If she does not like him that's not our fault. No one can say I ever set her against him."

"It was not necessary. She is friendly enough, but nothing more."

"Just so. And mark me," continued Mr. Harding, roughly to his wife, "I won't have you showing off airs to him. I don't want to quarrel with Kharapet. He is a devilish dangerous customer. I just want to keep quiet till Stasie is of age. It's far and away better for her not to marry till she is twenty-one, and got her affairs in her own hands. Husbands are the deuce and all to deal with. So let us go cannily to work ; and mind what I say, none of your cool stand-off airs to Kharapet."

Mrs. Harding's delicate cheek coloured faintly. She never could get quite accustomed to her husband's ruggedness ; his brutality degraded her in her own eyes. In pursuance of her resolution to assert herself, she made a brave effort to reply, while her heart beat hard. "You might say so with quite as much effect, and yet less rudely," she said. "As to my manner, I am always civil, and shall be. By the by," with a change of tone, and wishing to conciliate, "I had a very nice letter from Johnnie to-day. He is greatly improved in his writing," and she took it from her pocket to give him.

"Ha!" exclaimed Mr. Harding, whose face had expressed blank surprise at her words, "That's right. It is a great advantage, a clear, legible hand. The boy will turn out well, though you think him a dunce."

"More idle than dull. I too begin to hope

he will do well. I am so glad I persuaded you to let him go to school."

" You persuaded me! Gad, that's good! Why, it was my idea!"

Mrs. Harding wisely declined to dispute the point. She smiled pleasantly, and said, " Ah! very well," glancing at her book again.

" What are you reading? " asked Mr. Harding aggressively.

" An old quarterly Mr. Robinson lent me."

" It would better beseem you to be doing needlework for the children or the house, trying to save my poor pocket, instead of muddling your brains with what you can't understand, d—— me if you can! Besides, a man wants some one to talk to when he comes home."

" I never neglect either house or children; but I should be more ready to talk to you if you could speak as civilly to me as you do to Stasie Verner for instance."

" To Stasie Verner! By George! I believe you are jealous!" with a coarse laugh, partly because he was struck with his wife's words, and wished to hide the impression, partly because he had a proposition to make of which he was a little ashamed.

Mrs. Harding made no reply beyond a slight smile, and Mr. Harding resumed: " I have asked Kharapet to dinner on Friday, and I am going to ask Warden to meet him."

" Warden ? " repeated Mrs. Harding reflecting, " not Mr. Alfred Warden of that shipowning house ? "

" Yes ; why not ? " returned her husband, frowning heavily.

" Because he is not fit to sit at table with respectable people. It is not a year since the papers were full of the details of his disgraceful conduct to his wife ; and now he lives openly with another woman."

" Bah ! You are always on the side of the wives. There is no knowing what provocation he received ; and as to his dining here, it is a matter of business. I'll stand no d—d nonsense, I say he shall."

" I cannot, of course, prevent your bringing him into the house," replied Mrs. Harding firmly; " but I will not sit at table, nor will I receive him." She was a little surprised at her own courage, but the consciousness that she had a capital cause for holding her ground encouraged her.

Harding, after an astonished pause, burst out into furious language. " How dared she contradict him ! She, a beggar, who had never contributed a penny to their joint expenditure ! If she would not admit his friends into his house, she had better quit it. He *would* be master."

" I should not mind quitting it in the least," said she coolly, " as you must very well know ; but I maintain that I have a right to keep my children's home free from the presence of persons unfit to associate with them or me. Understand me distinctly, I will not meet this man ; nothing short of physical force will bring me into his presence, and *you* will not dare to make a scene for the sake of putting yourself in the wrong."

" In the wrong ! What do I care what any-one thinks," roared Mr. Harding, all the more fiercely that he felt his spirit quailing before the quiet firmness of his wife, which he so little expected.

" Yes, you *do* care ; every one cares for the opinion of those they live among. If you *must* entertain this repulsive man, why, ask him to meet Mr. Kharapet at some restaurant in town, though I should not have supposed any gentleman would care to have him as an acquaintance."

"That is all infernal bosh ! A dinner at a restaurant, indeed, just like your damned extravagance ! I warn you, Livy, that you are raising up a barrier between us that—that it will be hard to overcome."

"Why, *you* have been building up a barrier between us for nearly twelve years," returned his wife, in the same quiet voice, "and if you persist in bringing this man into the house you will complete it."

"What do you mean ? I think you have lost your senses ! "

"I am regaining them. I have no wish to irritate you unnecessarily. But I wish you to understand distinctly that I will *not* receive Mr. Warden, whatever may be the consequences. If you shut your eyes to what is right, it is my duty to open them ; and, pray, remember that as head of the house under you, and mother of your children, I ought to be, and I will be, a domestic power with which you must reckon."

As she said this slowly and distinctly, she looked him straight in the eyes, and from hers all the bitterness and resentment of her miserable life seemed to flash in one intense electric wave which swept down his meaner spirit, as the rising tide forces back the poor ripple of a stream.

Mr. Harding was stunned, he sat silent, openmouthed, while his wife rose and left the room, a new and agreeable sensation of relief and success thrilling through her veins.

She had made her first stand, and never would she yield an inch again.

She had, indeed, made a deeper impression than she was aware of. Mr. Harding lit a cigar, and pondered the whole matter profoundly.

His wife's opposition had been so astounding that his anger was stilled, and he reluctantly admitted that should they come to an open quarrel, the world *would* be on her side. Moreover, by a mental process very common with natures such as his, her self-assertion raised her at least twenty-five per cent in his estimation. He was not aware of being a bad husband, he did not deliberately mean to be good or bad. He was, on the whole, rather proud of his wife, but he had failed to make a thoroughly good bargain in his marriage, for he might have had money had he looked for it. His vanity was enormous, yet uneasy, and he was absolutely stupefied in some directions with selfishness. Still the world's opinion had great weight with him, and he felt it would not do to quarrel openly with Livy. Some extraordinary devilish spirit of obstinacy had seized her, probably it would not last, and then she would be sadly (he thought "dully") submissive as ever ; meantime it would not do to make a row in that little gossiping place, so he pulled out his pencil and note-book, and finally fell asleep over a calculation of what a dinner at Verey's would cost for three.

. . . . .

The next morning was bright and sweet, a faint silvery haze hung over the distant uplands, and a delicious crispness gave indescribable life to the air. Having accomplished her usual morning tasks, Mrs. Harding put on her hat and strolled through the garden to the road, and so on to ask for news of Stasie at Limeville.

She had heard no more of the projected dinner from her husband. He had said very little, but he had not been actively rude, and

she thought gravely of her position, and how to
make the best of it. She had quite lived through
the intolerable bitterness of finding out on what
merest, coarsest clay the pleasant outside colouring of her husband's *bonhomie*, frank hospitality,
and manly simplicity were lacquered. She had
gradually hardened in the cruel fire of experience
from the loving sensitiveness which shrunk from
a harsh word as from a blow to a quiet cynicism
which was nearly impervious; but nothing could
efface the strong necessity of circumstances
which demanded that for her children's sake she
should no longer lie helpless at their father's
feet to be trampled on. This conviction had
been growing on her, but was suddenly brought
into active motive power by Brooke's energetic
counsels. She found, too, on looking into her
own heart that time had been forging weapons
for her. With the shield of indifference, the
spear of true, fearless words, the reserve force of
self-reliance, she was prepared for conflict. But
what a life, what a destiny hers had been!
Nearly twelve years of loneliness, of repression,
of harshness and contempt, varied by fits of
fondness, degrading and loathsome in their un-

reasoning contrast, for what ? to weld and fuse the ingredients of her nature to a temper fitted to struggle for bare existence ? What had she done to deserve it?

Conscience answered "nothing;" she had simply made the ordinary everyday error of mistaking shadow for reality.

How much more bitterly ignorance or inno- cence is often punished than crime ; under the terrible rule of law there is no mercy, and the high court of equity has but a limited jurisdiction in life. She was little over thirty ; many a long year in all probability stretched its weariness before her. It was an arid outlook, but not quite denuded of verdure. She had the future of her children to live for and in. For their sakes she must be brave and strong. That she could raise or improve her husband she never now hoped for an instant; there was in him no material to work upon ; but she began to believe that he might be kept in better order. She quite longed to be able to tell Jim Brooke of the success attending her first attempt.

"Miss Stretton is working in the morning- room 'm," said the servant who opened the door.

"Do not disturb her; ask if I may go to her there."

"Come in, dear Mrs. Harding," cried Miss Stretton, who heard her voice. "Come and look at my work."

Mrs. Harding found her tied up in a large coarse apron, a huge paste-brush in her hand, a pile of bright-coloured pictures on a table beside her, and in front a high screen of three panels, which she was decorating to the best of her ability.

"What do you think of it? There is a terrible draught from that large window in the drawing-room, and I thought I would surprise Stasie when she came back."

"Very nice indeed! Do not let me interrupt you! Give me a pair of scissors. I can cut out some pictures while I talk to you," drawing off her gloves.

"Oh, thank you! You are a dear creature! there are the scissors; would you mind just cutting the foliage of 'The Lovers' Tryst' carefully. It will be a pretty contrast to this Harlequin and Columbine! one being coloured and the other not is no matter; indeed it makes a greater variety; a thing of this kind ought to be quite careless and irregular." So saying, she proceeded to affix poor Columbine and her companion in a perilous slant.

"And what news have you from Stasie?"

"Oh! excellent. I had quite a long letter from her this morning! Would you mind putting your hand in my pocket (mine are so sticky!); I think I put it in there. No! then I locked it up with the key-basket. Never mind, I can tell you all about it. She has been dining out, and making excursions, and going to croquet parties, and I don't know what; that young Pearson seems to be down there perpetually; depend upon it, Lady Pearson knows how to play her cards! Look, Mrs. Harding, shall I put this beautiful cock with the red feathers here?"

"No, he would look as if he were perched on the lover's head; put him a little to the right."

"Well, I fancy they are doing their best at Southsea to spoil Stasie. All that excitement and adulation really is not good for so young a girl; but she has a true noble heart; she is just as deeply interested in me, in you, every one, as if she were in some dull quiet place. Indeed, in her last she says—' every one is kind, and everything delightful, yet I shall not be sorry to be at home once more.'"

"Does she say so?" observed Mrs. Harding, as she began to clip the surrounding white paper from the picture of a splendid imperial *cent garde.* "She would never write that unless she felt it, and yet there is little to attract or amuse here."

"I am sure I don't know," returned Miss Stretton with vague mysteriousness. "There is no accounting for young girls' fancies. *I* shall be very glad to have her back at any rate, and I am happy to say she is ever so much better and stronger."

"I don't fancy this place agrees with her. We shall see how she is after her return. I am not sorry my cousin, Dr. Brooke, is coming to stay here, for he will be able to see more than we can, and let me know what he thinks without alarming her."

"Dr. Brooke coming to stay down here!" cried Miss Stretton, pausing with uplifted brush in hand, in great surprise. "To stay with *you,* I suppose?"

" No, with his friend Mr. Robinson."

"Most extraordinary," ejaculated Miss Stretton, fastening on "Romeo and Juliet," back uppermost.

"I think it is very natural," returned Mrs. Harding calmly. "He has business in London, and I suppose it must be more agreeable for him to be with his old friend than to be alone in a lodging."

"Of course! of course, and much more agreeable to you too, dear Mrs. Harding, to have a relative near you."

"Very agreeable indeed," said Mrs. Harding unconsciously.

"And pray when was this arranged?" asked Miss Stretton in a slightly peculiar tone.

"I don't know. Mr. Harding told me last night."

"I wonder what Mr. Kharapet will say."

"Nothing! what is it to Mr. Kharapet?" asked Mrs. Harding a little sharply.

"Well, you see Mr. Kharapet is so completely one of us."

"I do not admit that, and even if he were?"

"Oh! I am sure it is nothing to me," returned

Miss Stretton—a slippery illogical style of answer peculiar to ladies of her intellectual order, "only as Dr. Brooke's religious views are rather—confused—to say the least." She paused.

"Residence with so sound a churchman as Mr. Robinson will help to disentangle them," put in Mrs. Harding carelessly. "When does Stasie talk of returning?"

"Oh, not for quite ten days more. Mrs. Dalzell, Lady Pearson's daughter, is going to give a dance, and she wishes to wait for it."

"She is right! She ought to seize what pleasure she can, while she can!"

"Ah! my dear Mrs. Harding, pleasure is not the sole end of life."

"No, but one of its objects; can you imagine anything so horrible as life without pleasure?"

Miss Stretton was not fond of argument, and changed the conversation, which, however, did not flow very freely.

"Pray come and join the children and myself at our high tea this evening," said Mrs. Harding, rising and depositing her last feat in cutting out on the table. "Mr. Harding will be very late, and the children will be delighted to see you."

"Sweet darlings! I shall be charmed!" returned Miss Stretton.

.   .   .   .   .

When Brooke, the following day, conveyed himself and his personal luggage to Sefton Park, he was conscious of a little more lightness or perhaps revived strength of spirit than he had experienced since the evening on which he had suffered from the sensations we have described.

He had taken the first step in the struggle he intended to maintain against the attempt which he felt was being made upon Stasie Verner's life. He had gained a good position. He must now do his best to be wise as a serpent if harmless as a dove. He must on no account rouse Kharapet's suspicions, for the gentle Syrian, Brooke felt convinced, held the means of ending the strife at any moment he deemed necessary. Still, it was clearly his interest to work slowly. In this lay Brooke's only hope.

Sometimes he stopped himself, and asked if it were possible that a man of Kharapet's standing and seeming could conceive and execute so base a crime? Could it be Bhoodhoo's independent villainy? Might he not belong to that strange sect whose religion expressed itself in assassination? But a fanatic of this type would not cross the black water. No; he could only be a tool. Even so, how could he be so inhuman as to attempt the life of a creature who had loaded him with kindness. At this point Brooke generally checked himself for letting his thoughts wander about in a silly, sentimental, feminine style. What had he to do save with facts; and that the sweetmeat he had eaten was poisoned he did not—could not—doubt.

The day after his arrival he was early afoot, and made his way as soon as was permissible to see Mrs. Harding.

Here both enjoyed a long and confidential talk, at least it was thoroughly confidential on Mrs. Harding's side. It was a new and delightful pleasure to her to open her heart to so safe a counsellor as Brooke. He was sympathetic, but just, and quite alive to the necessities of her position. No hard words were said of the family tyrant; but the wisest mode of dealing with him was very frankly discussed, and the friends in council agreed that the horizon showed something of a gleam of light, especially as Mr.

Harding had announced that morning in a more than usually rugged and overbearing manner, that, after all, it would not do to drag men accustomed to their comforts down to a rough rascally hole like theirs, so he would just ask Warden to dinner at Greenwich or the Crystal Palace, " and be hanged to it.   I wish I had never broached the subject."

Mrs. Harding wisely made no remark, and accepted the dictatorial tone with which he sought to cover defeat, but the victory was to her.

The repose, the pure air, the sense of being on the scene of action brought a sense of relief to Brooke ; and perceiving that for some reason Mrs. Harding wished him to be on good terms with Miss Stretton, which corroborated him in his own intention, he next paid his respects at Lime-ville, where he was on the whole well received.

Miss Stretton hated to be alone. She had the liking for men's society which most women naturally feel, but in a stronger degree ; and when " Dr. Brooke" was announced she fled away upstairs with extraordinary agility to don a fresh and becoming contrivance of lace and ribbon—a sort of ornamental adaptation of middle age.

In the absence of Kharapet she found Brooke quite charming and entertaining, at very little cost to himself. He managed to listen to all she had to say with an air of deep interest, putting intelligent queries from time to time, which proved that he heard and understood, and collecting from her rambling discourse some gleams of additional light as to the conduct and probable views of Kharapet, which she little dreamed of affording.

He carefully avoided mentioning Stasie's name, but did not shut his ears when Miss Stretton held forth on that topic. He was cautious when the conversation turned on Mr. Harding. Yet, prepossessed as she was with a fixed idea on that subject, Miss Stretton's imagination, rather than her observation, found in his few and guarded words " proof as strong as holy writ " of his deep and unfortunate attachment to his cousin, who, " nice and sweet as she is, is really rather imprudent," concluded Miss Stretton in her own mind.

" It is very nice for your cousin, Mrs. Harding, having you down here for a while," said Aunt Clem, as Brooke was taking his leave.

" It is very nice for me to see a little more of her than I otherwise should, but I fancy she is so taken up with house and children that outsiders are of small importance to her."

Here his attention was attracted by something rubbing softly against his leg, and looking down, he perceived Stasie's little dog.

" Hollo, Pearl ! " he exclaimed, picking up the little creature. " What is the matter ? You are by no means in firstrate condition."

In truth, the dog had the indescribable rough poor look in his coat, which is a sure sign of neglect or indisposition ; his eyes were inexpressibly pathetic, and the eagerness with which he whimpered and strove to lick Brooke's hands or face said as plain as a dog could say, " A friend at last ! "

" He is quite well," said Miss Stretton ; " but he has been a naughty disobedient dog since Stasie went away, so he has been kept downstairs. Indeed, I am always a little afraid of him since he tried to bite poor dear Mr. Kharapet."

" I suspect the little beggar is sick for want of sympathy," returned Brooke, laughing, " let me take him out for a walk and try and get up his condition before Miss Verner comes back."

" I am sure I do not know when that will be," said Miss Stretton ; " she talks of staying another fortnight."

" And she is right ; sea air will set her up. Good-morning, Miss Stretton."

It gave Brooke a curious sense of pleasure to have Stasie's little favourite under his care. The springs of tenderness which in his character lay deep down under the superincumbent strata of pride and firmness, ambition and a thin seam of hardness, had been reached by the profound and generous pity which pierced through all. Full of thoughts respecting the task before him, of vivid memories of Stasie herself—her sweetness, her variety, her grace, and attractiveness—he strolled on and on, across the dull gray yellow of stubble fields, through plantations where the ground was red with fallen beech leaves, and over the corner of a wide breezy common. It was delicious to be in the country—the fresh crisp air gave him new vigour ; he would yet come off victorious and defeat the machinations of that villain Kharapet. Here the little terrier stopped and whined.

"Ha! Pearl, tired, little chap? I have forgotten what a scrap you are." He took up the tiny creature and carried it kindly, thinking, more or less clearly, till he drew near his temporary home. "This is a great improvement on deserted London," he said to himself, as he paused where the byeroad leading to Sefton Park turned off, "and at least I can enjoy it in peace while Stasie Verner is away. From what her aunt says, she is safe for at least a fortnight or ten days."

Even as the thought formed itself in his brain, a rusty-looking carriage, which he had heard approaching for some minutes, passed him, coming from Welwood.

As it passed at a tolerably good pace, he could hardly believe his eyes; and yet he could not doubt, that in it sat Miss Verner and another female figure. His heart gave a great throb. Her unexpected return at the very moment he was congratulating himself on her safety at a distance seemed like an evil omen. What unlooked-for event could have driven her back into the toils?

CHAPTER IV.

WHEN Lady Pearson recovered from the first
stunning effect of the terrible telegram respecting
her son's accident, her only thought was to fly to
him as fast as express trains could carry her, and
soon the whole household was preparing for her
departure.

Sir Frederic had unfortunately gone from
home for a few days' shooting, and young Pearson could not let his mother undertake such a
journey alone.

Mrs. Dalzell therefore took charge of Stasie,
and, though kind and thoughtful in spite of her
own distress, made no objection to her young
guest's proposal to return home at once.

The only train by which Stasie could conveniently travel was one on the main line. It
stopped at Welwood somewhere about five o'clock,
and Mrs. Dalzell insisted on sending her own

maid as Stasie's escort. Country telegrams were uncertain, she said, and Miss Verner must not be left to find her way alone in the dusk.

Stasie parted with sincerest sympathy and hearty regret from her kind hosts. She was deeply grieved for them. The thought of her own pleasures all cut short did not occur to her.

She kept picturing in her own mind what Lady Pearson must feel and suffer on her long sad journey. She earnestly prayed that she might find her boy not fatally injured, and that Mr. Pearson might be able to send her a tolerably good account. With her usual impulsiveness she had begged him to let her know how his mother had borne the journey, and how they found the sufferer.

Withal, she felt a certain sense of pleasure in drawing near her home. How pleased Aunt Clem would be to see her, and what delight to describe her experiences to Mrs. Harding—almost as delightful as the experiences themselves. Then a little thought, a tiny point of interrogation lit up in her mind : was Dr. Brooke still in London, and if so, did he often come down to Sefton

Park? From this, however, she turned reso-
lutely, and began to talk to her companion as
they drove homewards; thus she missed seeing
Brooke, who stood aside to let the cab pass.

It was past six; the gas was lit, and tea was
spread in the dining-room, where a small bright
fire had been kindled just to take off the feeling
of loneliness, Aunt Clem said to herself, when
the unwonted sound of wheels on the gravel
sweep before the front door arrested her hand as
she was about to measure out the tea, and Mary's
as she was hanging the kettle-stand on the bar
of the grate—

"Good gracious! What can it be, Mary?"
ejaculated Miss Stretton, not without alarm.

"Goodness knows,'m; there is the bell, and
Bhoodhoo's out, or he might be a help," replied
Mary, who probably thought "a man's a man for
a' that," whatever his colour, in a moment of
danger.

"Go and see who it is," rejoined Miss Stretton
with composure.

Mary disappeared, and soon a cheerful cry of
"Law,'m, here's Miss Verner!" reached Miss
Stretton's astonished ears.

" Stasie, my darling child ! How is this ? I am *so* glad to see you ; and who——" a pause.

"Oh ! this is Mrs. Dalzell's maid. We must make her as comfortable as we can to-night ; she is to return to-morrow. Mary, take Miller downstairs and give her a nice tea. Come in, auntie —Mary will see to the boxes—and I will tell you all about everything."

" At all events, dearest Stasie, I am charmed to have you back so soon, whatever the reason of your coming."

Amid many ejaculations from Aunt Clem, Stasie recounted the event which led to her unexpected return.

" Poor Lady Pearson ! What an awful blow !" cried Miss Stretton in a voice from which she could not banish a tone of satisfaction, so delighted was she to have her niece safe back again from the dangerous whirl of pleasure into which she had been plunged, and looking so well too —so heart-whole.

" I do hope the poor young man will recover."

" Yes, I earnestly hope he will. I dare say I shall hear something to-morrow or next day. I asked Mr. Pearson to be sure to write."

" What ! to write to you ? " Stasie nodded.

" My love, that was scarcely *comme il faut.*"

" I never thought about it ; and in such a case it surely could not matter. How else was I to hear anything ? "

" Through Mrs. Dalzell ; or you might have asked Mr. Pearson to write to *me.*"

" Oh, auntie ! that would have been too silly. I will go and take off my things, I feel so tired and dusty ; I shall be quite glad of a cup of tea."

" Go to my room, Stasie, dear. Yours is all covered up. Of course, nothing is ready," called Miss Stretton after her as she ran upstairs.

It was all rather bewildering to Stasie—this sudden return, this sudden dropping of a black curtain over the brightness, the movement, the soothing, flattering atmosphere in which she had lived for more than a fortnight ; yet she was pleased to see how genuinely glad Aunt Clem and Mary had been at her coming. It was really like coming home to find faces brightening at sight of her ; then, finding herself in the familiar room made her think of the wonderful improvement in her own health. How strong and well she felt ! all her accustomed hopefulness and sense of physical ease had come back to her. The delicious sea air had set her up. True, she would miss the gaiety of her surroundings to-morrow ; but there would be Mrs. Harding to talk to ; perhaps Dr. Brooke might come down sometimes, and that would be a variety—at least he had always something to say that was worth hearing. If she were only on sufficiently intimate terms with him to question him on many topics she longed to talk about, how much she would gain ! but she was not, and she feared to bore him.

It was not worth while to do her troublesome hair over again, she would go to bed early, and have it properly brushed out, so she smoothed it over, or tried to do so, pulled the lace round her neck straight, and went away to join her aunt.

On opening the dining-room door, to her great surprise, a tall gentleman was standing face to face with Aunt Clem, to whom he was saying, " so I took the liberty of coming in to assure myself."

" There she is to answer your queries," replied Miss Stretton, who was still decked in smiles.

The next instant Stasie's hand was in Dr. Brooke's. She was startled by the eager questioning of his eyes, as he looked into hers, and seemed to search into her soul. She was girlishly annoyed that her hair was in such disorder, that her dress was not carefully arranged. She did not think how sweet and fair she seemed to him, with the renewed colour of health on her cheek, and the rich confusion of her golden brown hair.

"How is it you are here?" cried Stasie in frank surprise, and in no way confused by his gaze, which was simply anxious—not tender or admiring, or in the faintest degree lover-like.

"I was walking on the Welwood Road," he returned, "and caught sight of you as you passed. I could hardly believe my eyes. I know you were not expected for some time, so I ventured to call in order to allay my curiosity."

Stasie explained the cause of her return, and, while she spoke, the whining and scratching of Pearl attracted her attention.

"You little dear!" catching him up, "I am ashamed of myself. I quite forgot to ask for you. Poor Lady Pearson's trouble put nearly everything else out of my head."

" I did not fancy Pearl looked very flourish-
ing, and I took him out for a walk," said Dr.
Brooke.   " I fear I made him go too far ; he was
evidently tired, so I carried him home."

" How good of you ! " said Stasie.   " Do you
know, I do not think Pearl's coat looks as nice
as when I left.   I am afraid he is not a favourite
with you, Aunt Clem."

" Will you not join us at our evening meal,
Dr. Brooke ? " asked Aunt Clem blandly.

" No, I thank you ; I cannot stay.   But I
must congratulate you, Miss Verner.   I see that
change has worked wonders for you.   You look
like what you were when we first met—ages
ago, was it not ?   That is, four or five months
ago.   Yet it seems in some strange way a cycle
—at least to me."

" And to me too, but then the change from
school accounts for that.   Yes, I am much better,
quite well, in fact."

" We must see that you do not fall back,"
returned Brooke.   " I have a strong impression
this place does not suit you."

Here the door opened to admit Bhoodhoo,
who brought the toast-rack, and advanced with a

low salaam, a joyous expression beaming on his dark face, and glittering in his black eyes.

"Good-evening, Bhoodhoo, have you been quite well?" said Stasie kindly.

"Quite well, but much better now since missee Sahib come back! No sunshine when missee away. No curries to make—nothing!"

"Thank you, Bhoodhoo! You must make me a curry to-morrow."

"I will, missee, beautiful good curry;" and with another salaam Bhoodhoo retreated.

"I really think poor Bhoodhoo is quite fond of me," said Stasie, looking after him with a smile.

"He ought to be," remarked Aunt Clem solemnly, "and he is certainly very useful." Brooke said nothing. He seemed to Stasie plunged in a sudden fit of deep thought.

In truth he was for a moment silenced, over-whelmed by a horror that laid its sudden grip upon him, as Bhoodhoo approached Stasie with his soft false smile, and she was so bright, so kind, so unsuspecting! Had she indeed recovered her full strength only to come back into the jaws of death? and he, great heavens! how helpless, how very nearly helpless he was to save her!

A cold ripple shivered through his veins, and it was with an effort he roused himself to bid both ladies good-evening. " I shall see you to-morrow if I may call," he said. " I should like to hear some account of your plunge in the gay world, Miss Verner."

" Well, auntie," said Stasie after he had gone, as she stirred her tea meditatively, "if *I* have recovered since I saw Dr. Brooke, I think he has fallen off. Does he not look very ill ? "

One does not notice a change much in those sort of thin, dark, grave men, but now you mention it, he *does* look ill."

" But how does he happen to be here, auntie, so late, and——"

" My dear, it is all rather mysterious ! He is staying with Mr. Robinson, actually living there ; and what attraction a place of this sort can have for a man of the world like Dr. Brooke, who is fond of his club and men's society, and is quite different from Mr. Robinson (indeed, I cannot understand how they are such friends) — what attraction Sefton Park can have for such a man, I cannot imagine. In short, there can be but one."

"And that?" asked Stasie, though she felt pretty sure what the answer would be.

"Well, my dear, it is with great reluctance I say it, and I am sure a breath of such a suspicion should never cross my lips to mortal save yourself, but I cannot help seeing that Dr. Brooke is deeply attached to Mrs. Harding. Mind, I do not accuse her of encouraging him! She *may* be unconscious (though I doubt it!) but I have not the smallest doubt that this wonderful friendship with Mr. Robinson is just to get near her; and his great interest in your health! it is all part of a plan; and my own real opinion is that the sooner he goes back to India the better!"

Stasie mused. What more likely than that the old tenderness for his charming cousin should have revived with fresh vigour, especially when he perceived the terrible life of isolation and repression to which she was doomed! That she was conscious of anything save simple kindly friendship, for which she was innocently grateful, nothing would ever make her (Stasie) believe. But Brooke? how would it be with him? He must be very unhappy. Ah! how sweet to have the disinterested, faithful devotion of a strong thoughtful man such as he was. "I think, auntie, you must imagine a great deal. Pray, pray be prudent. I am as sure as that I live that Mrs. Harding does not for a moment dream of anything save the purest, simplest friendship."

"We will hope so, at any rate," said Miss Stretton with prudent reservation.

Stasie took her tea in silence, while Aunt Clem, thinking that her niece was really improved in habits of attention, continued to pour forth a vast quantity of accumulated gossip. Little of it, however, reached Stasie's ears. Though she did her best to disregard her aunt's suggestions respecting Mrs. Harding and Brooke, they sank deep into her heart. Perhaps the worn, uneasy expression she had noticed in Brooke's face was to be accounted for by some internal struggle. The idea rather recommended itself to her romantic fancy; as for any evil arising out of it, that possibility never entered her head. She pictured to herself Brooke, always silently devoted to Mrs. Harding and her children, growing renowned in his profession, returning perhaps from India ultimately a gray-haired, low-spirited, elderly gentleman, who would treat little Ethel as a daughter, and leave her heir to all he possessed.

Here the vision of Brooke, as he was in the flesh, square, erect, cool, keen, the very antithesis of everything sentimental, rose before her, and she smiled at her own idea.

He was not the man to waste himself in despair, or die " because a woman's fair." Yet, if he ever did love !——

Well, what was it all to her ? How foolish to spend brain power in pondering these things ! how weak and dreamy she was !

" Good-night, dear Aunt Clem ! It is quite nice to have a talk with you again ; but I *am* so sleepy."

.   .   .   .   .

Though many an anxious, almost despairing, day and night were yet to be encountered by Brooke, perhaps none of them surpassed in torment this first plunge into the reality of his position. To think that he was obliged to leave Stasie without warning, without an attempt to preserve her, at the mercy of that wretched tool of Kharapet's (Heaven alone knew what devilish decoction he might not be at that moment brewing to sap his young mistress's life), was almost unbearable. That unforeseen circumstances should have so favoured Kharapet's design as to cut short the breathing space of safety on which he had reckoned seemed an indication full of evil omen. How should he shape his course?

Then Stasie herself, once more blooming with the perfect health he so much admired, so bright, so kindly, had deeply and freshly touched him. The conviction that through him was her sole means of escape, that he was her only efficient protector, affected him powerfully. He was resolved to win her if possible ; and so, resigning all effort at self-mastery, he permitted his thoughts to dwell upon her, living over again each moment he passed with her since her indescribable reserve had begun to pique his curiosity.

What a task lay before him ! Stasie was no mere romantic schoolgirl, to be had for the asking ! And, after all, might she not prefer the youth and brightness of young Pearson, which resembled her own ? Even that he could bear, maddening as it would be to give her up to another ; but could he be sure her marriage would take place in time to prevent the completion of Kharapet's intended crime? But he knew it would not. The guardian's consent must be obtained, and the guardian was wandering in inaccessible places even then. Pearson might easily be induced to wait six months—a year —and before the expiration of that period Stasie would be in the cold grave.

Her only safety lay in marriage, immediate marriage with himself. And he must work alone unaided, unless, indeed, he could secure an ally in Sir Harcourt Filmer !

"My dear Brooke, what is the matter? You have been pacing the room for the last half hour and more, with the aspect of a man ' on desperate deeds intent.' "

"I beg your pardon, Robby; I am afraid I am anything but a cheerful visitor. I did not know I wore such a villainous aspect. The fact is, I have a good deal to think about just now ; it is not easy to make up one's mind on a question of great importance without a good deal of reflection "—he paused—" and reflection *will* come, in and out of season. Come, Robinson, do you ever play cards or chess or humbler backgammon ? I don't want either to talk or think."

"I have a chess-board and men, but I am a most indifferent player. If you are one of those impatient fellows that cannot put up with mediocrity you will be smashing the board after a short trial of me."

"No, I shall not!" returned Brooke, smiling; "patience is a special virtue of mine. I have carefully cultivated it, and I do not think you will find me a formidable antagonist to-night."

They played for some time in silence, but Robinson observed that Brooke's thoughts were not on his game; he even lost with equanimity beyond what might have been expected even from a patient man. The second game was drawn out to great length, but Brooke was the victor. He made no attempt to replace the pieces; and Robinson, who was quite proud of having held his own so well, asked if they should try for a conqueror.

"No, thank you! You are quite my match, Robby, to-night, at least." Robinson proceeded obediently to put the pieces away.

"When did you say Kharapet was coming down here?" asked Brooke suddenly, as if out of his thoughts.

" I do not know exactly. Miss Stretton mentioned that he would come when Miss Verner returned."

Brooke growled something inarticulate, but not amiable. " I am often surprised that enlightened men like yourself have such strong prejudices on the subject of race and colour," said Mr. Robinson in reply to the growl. " You bristle up at the sound of Kharapet's name; now he really is a very nice fellow."

" But I am not prejudiced," returned Brooke. " I think I know Easterns pretty well, and I like them better than most Englishmen do. They have many good points we do not possess; they are sympathetic and full of tact — an admirable quality, which ought to rank higher than it does; then their intelligence is of a high order, though moulded on very different lines from ours; their heads are very differently shaped; still I can get on with Easterns, but I dislike Kharapet, individually; I distrust him, and I would not have you too trusting, Robby——"

" But how could he hurt me ? " exclaimed Robinson. " He couldn't rob me, for I have no money to lose, and I don't suppose he would murder me, ch ? "

" No," said Brooke slowly, as if to himself. " No, there is nothing to gain in murdering *you.*"

" I protest you are too bad, Brooke ! " cried Robinson, laughing. " Have some brandy and soda, and let us go to bed."

.   .   .   .   .

The morning light brought renewed courage and resolution to Brooke. He must keep his head clear, his nerves steady, or he could do nothing. He went early into town, travelling in the same carriage with Mr. Harding, who was quite cordial and talkative on various subjects, and finally invited Brooke to take " pot luck " with him the following day.

The object of Brooke's visit to London was to ascertain if Sir Harcourt Filmer had returned to town, and if not, when he was expected to return. Sooner or later, he must have recourse to the aid of the great M.D. He, at least, with his wide experience, would enter into Brooke's terrible suspicions—nay, certainty—and help him. He longed intensely to be able to speak to some one of the load which oppressed him.

But Filmer was still absent, and not expected back for a week or ten days.

There was nothing for it then but to be brave, self-reliant, guarded. Whatever Kharapet's ultimate designs, he would not dare to execute them quickly.

Meanwhile, Stasie was away as soon as breakfast was over to enjoy a long talk with Mrs. Harding.

The children at the sound of her voice broke bounds and rushed out of the schoolroom to greet her, followed by Mademoiselle, who considered Mees Verner *charmante*.

"How pretty the park is looking!" cried Stasie, throwing aside her hat, as, the children having been recaptured, she settled herself for a nice long confidential talk with Mrs. Harding. "The trees look so rich and lovely after Southsea, which is very bare! But oh! was it not unfortunate that poor Frank Pearson met with that accident? It must have been a bad one, or they would not have telegraphed for Lady Pearson. Oh! Mrs. Harding! if you had seen the expression of her face! so terror-stricken, so strained, and think of the hours she must travel before she can know the truth about him! I am afraid I should bear up very badly if such a trial came to me; it is dreadful to be cowardly, and yet I do not think it is cowardice altogether."

"No, I do not think it is," said Mrs. Harding, smiling kindly. "I don't think you would fail at a pinch. But it was rather a pity that all your enjoyment was cut short."

"Yes! I am selfish enough to think of that too, but I am not sorry to be back with you, dear Mrs. Harding, and poor Aunt Clem! she was *so* delighted to see me! Yet life was uncommonly pleasant at Southsea; every one was so bright and easy, perfectly polite, and not a bit stiff; and I was quite spoiled, or would have been if I had not been well snubbed by dear Mrs. Mathews and the boys in my early days; it would take a great many fine speeches to persuade me I am an angel in the teeth of such recollections; yet I think all *did* like me"—a long pause, Stasie gazing, thoughtfully out of window at the lovely tints on the trees of a thicket in the hollow below the house. Then she resumed: "Tell me, dear Mrs. Harding, for I think you see things very clearly, were I quite

poor, that is like dear Ella Mathews, I mean
Mrs. Baldwin, do you think they would all make
such a fuss about me ? Aunt Clem says things
every now and then that make me feel vexed
and disgusted. Surely *some* people would love
me, even if I had nothing."

"They would undoubtedly, dear," cried Mrs.
Harding with warmth. "I should, and I believe
your aunt herself would, and many others; but
I doubt if people generally would make a fuss
about you. Lady Pearson is a kind good
woman, and is, I dare say, genuinely pleased with
you, but she would not ask you to her house and
encourage her son to be with you perpetually if
she did not think you would be a good match
for him. This is only natural; you need not
quarrel with her for that."

"I suppose not," said Stasie, her big wistful
eyes glittering with something very like unshed tears. "And Van Pearson, would he be as
pleasant and obliging and as ready to do everything in the world for me if I were quite poor."

"Oh! he might. He seems a nice, honest
young fellow, and I suppose has a young man's
weakness for a handsome girl; but—had you not

possessed the means of entering society on the same footing as himself, why—you would probably never have met, and if you had, prudence would have kept him from cultivating the acquaintance. Mr. Pearson will want more money than his father can leave him."

There was another pause, while Stasie managed to swallow her tears, for she had broached a subject that troubled her occasionally.

"Don't let me put you against young Pearson," resumed Mrs. Harding. "I like him, and I do not think (so far as I can judge) he would marry any woman he did not like, or let us say love, merely because she had money; but he cannot marry without it."

"How horrible and degrading it must be to be married only for one's money!" cried Stasie, with a sparkle of scorn in her eyes.

"It is quite as degrading to be married only for one's beauty, or what a man considers one's beauty," returned Mrs. Harding. "It is a charm that soon vanishes, and then," she paused expressively — Stasie was silent. "I like Mr. Pearson, and I think he is very fond of you, Stasie; do not mislead him, dear. I do not

mean to insinuate that you are a coquette, but—
you may be thoughtless."

"Do you mean to say I could ever think of
marrying Van Pearson?"

"You might do worse," returned Mrs. Harding, with a slight sigh.

"Why, my dear Mrs. Harding, he is a mere
boy. He hasn't as much sense as I have myself.
He ought not to think of marrying for seven or
eight years."

"He is twenty-five or twenty-six—years older
than you are."

"That is of little consequence when I don't
feel one bit of respect for him. He is nice, I
like him very, very much; but I will mind
what you say, for I should be so sorry to dis-
appoint him. I wish people were not always
thinking of marrying me. Aunt Clem is perpetually talking of it, and even *you*, who are so
kind and sensible, here you are holding forth on
the same topic."

"My dear Stasie, you led me into it yourself.
I believe that being free, and well off, your best
course would be to keep so."

Stasie was silent for a moment, and then

said softly and deliberately, " No, I do not fancy a lonely selfish life.   I should like to marry, but not for some years—a good many years.   Dear Mrs. Harding, I am very happy in general, and I know I ought to be ; but at times, not often, I feel a strange bitter pang when I think how lonely I am, for I belong to no one, and no one belongs to me.   I often wish I could have stayed with the Mathewses ; and then when I was ill, before I went to Southsea, I used to have such curious fits of despair.   Do you know, I felt very ill sometimes.   But now I am well and strong ; all this has passed away, and I see how thankful I ought to be to have kind friends, and enough money and health.   You will think me foolish ; indeed I feel I am, but——" she stopped abruptly, blushing and smiling.

" No, dear, not foolish ; only liable to low spirits like other people when physically out of sorts.   Don't dwell on such moods, they *will* come ; just put them aside and forget them as fast as you can."

Stasie jumped up, gave her a kiss, and, returning to her seat, obeyed at once by starting a fresh subject.

"I found poor, dear Pearl looking very ill. I am afraid he is not a favourite of Aunt Clem's since he snapped at Hormuz Kharapet. How very good it was of Dr. Brooke to take the little creature for a walk!"

"Yes, he has a wonderfully kind heart under a somewhat cold exterior. I am very pleased he has come down here to stay, though it surprises me a good deal."

"He likes to be near you, I suppose," said Stasie, feeling as if her question was so deeply Jesuitical that she ought to be ashamed of herself.

"No doubt he does," replied Mrs. Harding calmly. "Still that does not seem to me a sufficient reason. I think he is anxious and undecided about returning to India."

"Yes, he has a sort of careworn look. Do you think you could come with me for a long walk, Mrs. Harding, after luncheon to-day, round by Welwood and the Common?"

"I might be able, if I can finish some letters Mr. Harding left me to copy by two o'clock."

"I will come and see," replied Stasie; "but I must run away now."

CHAPTER V.

THE days which immediately followed Stasie's return were very pleasant ones to her, and to Brooke also they were sprinkled with happy moments when the sweetness of a first real passion —a passion purified by true tenderness—made him forget his haunting fears.

He was usually occupied in the mornings with a work he was preparing on some physiological subject of importance, and which he hoped might lay the foundation of future fortune, but the bright crisp autumnal afternoons were spent walking or driving with Mrs. Harding and Stasie through the pleasant picturesque country roads and lanes, and over breezy commons which were in the neighbourhood.

Kharapet's visit, which he had dreaded, made little difference to this mode of existence. The Syrian was very quiet and gentle, and scrupulously avoided anything like interference with any one. He was quite friendly to Brooke, who felt compelled to accept his advances with seeming readiness. The smooth-tongued, dark-eyed Hormuz held in his cruel grasp a tremendous weapon, the power of life or death over a creature who was rapidly twining herself with Brooke's every hope and anticipation. Any evidence of suspicion on his part would only increase Stasie's danger. Often Brooke's self-control was put to a terrible test, when perhaps the little circle of intimates were gathered in Miss Stretton's drawing-room of an evening, and Boodhoo would appear in his smartest clothes to wait specially on Stasie. Every cup of tea or coffee he handed to his kind young mistress sent a cold shiver of dread through Brooke's veins. God only knew what deadly mixture it contained! Only when Aunt Clem made tea in the room did he feel at ease. With what intense observation he watched Stasie, and each night as he was able to tell himself that he could see no change in the expression of her eyes—no acceleration of breathing—no irritability of manner—he thanked heaven and took courage. Time—time was all he asked—

time to win her! How he burned to carry her
away from all danger, to watch and tend her
himself, to pour out all the passion that swelled
his heart, to waken the love that lay dormant in
her rich generous nature, which some mysterious
influence seemed to have, not hardened against,
but veiled from him.

His very absorption in her, his deep serious
anxiety, were drawbacks to his progress as a lover.
He was too grave, too preoccupied for those
slight, graceful, contagious indications of feeling
that delicately suggest to a girl delicious possibilities of loving and being loved. Yet Stasie
deeply enjoyed her walks and conversations with
him. His gravity — the long, earnest, wistful
looks she caught at times fixed upon her—interested her in spite of her firm resolution to be
neither weak nor credulous. Brooke's preoccupied
and at times even melancholy manner she accounted for by supposing him warmly attached
to his cousin, and depressed by the hopelessness
of her fate, the unhappiness of her ill-assorted
marriage. Still, there were little incidents in
their daily intercourse which sometimes startled
other ideas from their slumbers in the inner

depths of her heart. The eager haste with which
he caught her once when her foot slipped in getting over a stile—the strong throbbing of his
heart when for a moment she was held against
it—the magic revelation of his lingering touch,
if by accident their hands met—all these " trifles
light as air " disturbed Stasie at intervals, though
she kept her self-mastery with wonderful strength
for so young a creature. She was in some indescribable way aware that she must not, dare not
yield to the longing that would spring up at the
least relaxing of the reins—the desperate longing
to be all and all to the man who on the slightest
deviation from his severe ideal of propriety coldly
backed out of the friendly intimacy which had
grown between them. Her pride perpetually
whispered, " Take care !"

Nevertheless, in spite of doubts and self-dis-
trust it was a very pleasant time ; and when Dr.
Brooke forgot his troubles to talk naturally and
easily, it was more than pleasant.

Meanwhile it was " fine times " also for Aunt
Clem. Kharapet was devoted to her, and Brooke
for his own reasons showed her much polite attention. She rose, therefore, considerably in her own

estimation (being unprovided with any scale of self-measurement, she generally adopted that of her associates), so all went well and tranquilly. No signs of disturbance such as he had before witnessed in Stasie appeared to arouse fresh terror in Dr. Brooke ; he was almost disposed to hope that Kharapet had renounced his murderous design, or could it be an independent villainy of Bhoodhoo's ? This notion had presented itself before, and been rejected.

.   .   .   .   .

Stasie's uneasiness respecting Lady Pearson and her son had been early relieved by a letter from her lancer friend, who was happy to report his brother's injuries not so serious as at first supposed. His leg was broken and he was much bruised, but with good nursing they hoped all would go well. Of course Lady Pearson would take the invalid to their house in town ; so the Southsea episode was over, but would long dwell in the writer's memory. His leave would soon expire, and then he hoped to see her again, as the detachment would probably remain some time longer at Hounslow.

"I shall be quite pleased to see him," said

Stasie to her aunt when she had finished reading aloud this epistle. "You don't know how nice he was in his mother's house !"

"Oh ! I daresay," rejoined Miss Stretton ; "but he has not the solidity of Dr. Brooke, nor the gentle unobtrusive kindness of Mr. Kharapet, the beauty of whose character grows upon one more and more." It was Miss Stretton's misfortune that she never could let well alone, nor listen to a eulogium on any one obnoxious to herself without uttering a qualification or a protest.

These little follies irritated Stasie like the bites of a midge, and had Aunt Clem been wealthy and strong she would have received some very rasping replies ; as it was, Stasie was far too chivalrous by nature to hurt what was weaker than herself, and generally met these small stings with silence.

Kharapet had spent a few days at Sefton Park, chiefly occupied in overlooking Aunt Clem's accounts, and putting them straight, creeping slowly round the garden, or through the kitchen and pantry, to talk with Bhoodhoo, who was profoundly respectful, smoking the pipes which that accomplished native contrived to "make" in spite of many difficulties, or playing draughts of an evening with Miss Stretton. He seemed tranquil and content; moreover, to Stasie's infinite relief, he appeared to have dropped all lover-like pretension; still her original hearty liking for him never returned, but on the surface they appeared as good friends as before. Kharapet was almost ostentatiously careful not to interfere in any way with Stasie's plans or movements, and occasionally, when Brooke went over to tea or luncheon at Limeville, Kharapet took the opportunity of enjoying a *tête-à-tête* discussion with Robinson on Biblical history and criticism. Indeed his society was very precious to the young incumbent, only at times he suggested uncomfortable doubts regarding passages which had previously seemed clear as light; still, except to Mr. Robinson and Miss Stretton, his departure was a relief. But only in a slight degree to Brooke, who felt that his presence or absence had but little effect on Stasie's safety. He found himself counting almost the hours, and congratulating himself that he had not as yet observed any change in the eyes he watched so

eagerly, yet furtively. How he longed to hold
fast the soft pinky white hand given to him at
least once every day, and gather from the pulse
some idea of the hidden action of heart and
blood !

It was a couple of days after Kharapet's
departure. Brooke had been in London during
the morning, and hurried back with his usual
fear of finding " something wrong " on his return,
which generally grew upon him when absent for
a few hours. He stopped at the parsonage to
leave some books he had brought with him, and
then, armed with an illustrated paper as an excuse, he called at Limeville. Both ladies were
out, the servant said ; they had driven over to
Welwood with Mrs. Harding, she believed.
Brooke left his paper, and strolled on to the top
of the hill, feeling unreasonably disappointed.
The Hardings' house was quiet, no shrill joyous
voices sounded from the garden or yard. He
paused a moment to look at the pleasant view
over the downward sweep of woodland, with a
church spire in the blue distance, and then
descended the steep road which led through the
side of the park as yet not built upon. It was a

still, soft, gray evening, with a faint tinge of autumnal melancholy in the atmosphere. Brooke felt unaccountably depressed. What was to be the end of this terrible time of trial ? Stasie had seemed in perfect health ever since her return from Southsea, though yesterday he had noticed her twice press her hand to her heart, but it might mean nothing.

Kharapet might hold his hand for a while, and then renew his attempts. Then he himself seemed to make no way with her ; she kept him at a distance by a wonderful calm, a steady self-possession that paralysed him ! He was not aware that the paralysis came from the intense anxiety that blinded his eyes, and in one direction dulled his perception. Again for the thousandth time he reviewed the position. To whom dare he whisper his suspicions ? Mr. Harding's crass selfishness would shut him out from the possibility of imagining any man such a cursed fool as to risk such a crime. Mrs. Harding, though she disliked the Syrian, would not for a moment believe him capable of it, nor the local doctor, nor Robinson, and Stasie herself least of all. Then what proof could he offer ?

Positively none. The effect of the helwa on himself—a dozen common-sense solutions might be offered to account for his symptoms, especially as he had swallowed nearly all the sweetmeat left with him, only twice feeling the same kind of effect, and that in a much less degree.

As he worked round and round the same painful circle of thought, he reached some sand-pits at the foot of the hill, and turning by a large oak-tree which overshadowed the cart track leading down to them, intending to take a path-way through the fields to the Welwood Road, he came suddenly upon Stasie Verner and paused to contemplate her strange employment.

Beside the road or rather track sprang a plentiful crop of nettles, and browsing upon them was a very miserable donkey, with de-sponding ears and a helpless-looking tail which he feebly twitched, trying to scare away the flies attracted by an open sore beside his back-bone. Stasie had laid down her sunshade and a little basket full of ferns which she had been uprooting, and was carefully laying a large cool dock leaf over the place, speaking tenderly to the wretched animal, who ate on unmoved.

Brooke stood still a moment to look on, half amused, half touched, and not aware that she perceived him, until without any greeting she said, "Do you think it will stick on?"

"I am afraid not, though it appears to adhere to the broken skin at present."

"Well, it will give the poor thing a little relief, and when night comes those horrid flies will not bite!" so saying, with a parting pat to the donkey, she took up her basket and sunshade, and turned her steps towards home.

"I heard you had all gone over to Welwood," said Brooke, keeping by her side.

"Mrs. Harding, Aunt Clem, and the children have; I only went as far as Ashby woods, and came through them to get these ferns; there are quantities of ferns there, and, I imagine, heaps of wild flowers in the spring. It will be delightful to walk there if we are still here."

"Where do you think you will be?"

"I have no idea—somewhere—anywhere. I think often I should like to have wings, to be perpetually in motion—it is a curious feeling," and she looked up at him with a smile.

Good God! with what a wild pang of horror

he observed that her eyes had something of the enlarged strained look he so dreaded. Her manner, too, was less calm; the way in which she played with the tassel of her sunshade seemed to him suspiciously restless and uneasy.

"It was a long lonely walk for you, Miss Verner; you ought to have had a companion."

"There is nothing to fear, except, they say, at the race time; then London tramps come about."

"Why did you not send for me? I am an idle man now, and very glad to be of use." He could hardly command himself to speak in his natural voice. He longed to clasp her to his heart, to implore her to let him take her away that very instant from danger, from death!

"Oh, I could not think of troubling you," said Stasie, little dreaming the struggle going on in her companion's heart. "You would not care to wander about woods rooting up ferns."

"Yes, I should," returned Brooke rather abruptly; "men of my calling are given to botanise, 'to cull simples,' as old-fashioned romances term it, and—and—at all events, now that we are good friends (are we not, Miss

Verner ?), I like a talk and an argument, as we used to have, four ages,—that is, four months ago, —even when I get the worst of it."

"But you never do get the worst," replied Stasie, laughing, "for even when I feel I am right, I never know how to prove it."

Thus talking, with frequent pauses, for Brooke recovered himself but slowly, they reached the house.

Brooke hesitated, " I left an *Illustrated London News* for you just now," he said ; "there are one or two admirable pictures of Welsh scenery in it. I should like to show them to you."

"Oh, come in," said Stasie, quite at her ease. "Aunt Clem will soon be back, and we are going to dine at Sefton House. Is it not a grand name for an old homestead?"

Brooke did not need a second invitation, and followed her into the drawing-room, where they found Bhoodhoo apparently occupied in sweeping up the hearth. Stasie gave him her basket and her hat ; then, sitting down as if tired on the sofa by the fireplace, drew her little work-table to her, and, leaning her elbow on it, she said,

"What a good useful creature Bhoodhoo is! He saves the other servants so much! he thinks of everything; I do believe he has been putting my work in order."

"Do you keep your supply of Syrian sweetmeats at hand there?" asked Brooke sharply.

"Sometimes," she returned, looking up much surprised.

"Have you any there now?"

"I had a few, but I see Bhoodhoo has put some more;" she took a piece and offered it to him.

"Give them all to me," cried Brooke, drawing a chair close to her, and gazing into her eyes as though he would pierce through the fleshly veil into the depths of her being. "I see that you have been eating this horrible stuff! Promise me you will not! You cannot hide from me that you are not yourself—not quite well."

"Do not look at me like that, Dr. Brooke," she exclaimed, covering her face with her hands. "I cannot bear it. I will not have you cross-examine me. You frighten me. You make me feel ill and uneasy. There is nothing the matter

—only—only the place does not agreee with me. I will go away, I will take Aunt Clem; we can go for the winter to the seaside, or—you do not think I am really seriously ill?" with a sudden change of tone.

"I would not frighten you for worlds," said Brooke, lowering his voice, and speaking with a tenderness of tone that stirred Stasie's heart strangely. "And, so far as I can judge, you have magnificent health; but just now you should be careful. You should have advice; you do not wish for mine; let me entreat you to consult a man of the highest skill, whose advice will, in all probability, enable you to overcome these unpleasant symptoms. Tell me, I beg you, this : have you felt your heart beat quickly, so quickly for a few moments that you feel breathless?"

"Not so bad as that; but yesterday I fancied it did beat faster than usual, and last night I could not sleep. Now, do not ask me any more questions, and do not think me rude," she went on in her most serious tone, all playful petulance banished. "If I do not want you to be—that is, to prescribe for me—I am sure you are very

clever, very; but you see you arc a friend whom
I meet every day, and if you were my doctor too
I should always fancy I was very ill, or getting
worse, or something of that kind, every time
you looked gravely at me; and you look awfully
grave sometimes, Dr. Brooke, almost unhappy."

"Almost!" repeated Brooke, "altogether!"
The words escaped his lips before he was well
aware of them. Perhaps they might produce an
effect favourable to his object in arousing Stasie's
notice of her own health, her interest in himself.
There was an indescribable, sweet frankness in
her voice and manner as she excused herself for
not seeking his professional aid; a dim delicious
idea suggested itself that her reluctance to accept
him as a physician might arise, perhaps, out of
the natural shrinking of a delicate girl from those
undraped communications which the relation of
patient and doctor compel, but which any dawning of warmer feelings forbid. If she could but
love him the battle would be won. He had
almost unconsciously risen and paced the room
while he thought. Stasie watched him with
wondering eyes. What could disturb him? What
could make him "altogether" unhappy?

"I quite understand you," he said, returning to his seat. "Many persons have a nervous dislike to the doctor's presence, save when it is absolutely necessary. I do not wish to intrude upon you ; but, in an outside way, let me advise you to give up eating helwa and all made dishes. You are not too dainty to dine on a plain joint, I hope ?" and he tried, not very successfully, to produce a playful smile.

"Oh ! I am not such a baby as to eat what I am told is bad for me," replied Stasie, who was much impressed with his manner. "But can there be much harm in helwa ? Poor Bhoodhoo would be quite mortified if I did not eat his sweeties."

"Do not mortify him, then. Give me some, put more in the fire, let him believe you take them ; but pray give them up for a while, and let me speak to Mrs. Harding about Filmer—I mean, about your consulting a first-rate man, a friend of mine."

"Very well," returned Stasie thoughtfully. "But I do not think this place suits me ; I was a different creature at Southsea."

Brooke was so deeply conscious of this fact—

so convinced in his own mind of its cause—that he did not trust himself to reply, and Stasie went on a little shyly, but always with a sweet honesty —"Do you know, Dr. Brooke, I do not think Sefton Park suits *you.* You look, I do not know exactly how, but worn and—and—you don't mind my saying it?—sad, melancholy, and rather stern, as if something was going wrong."

"Exactly," returned Brooke, resting one elbow on his knee, his cheek on his hand, thus bringing his eyes on a level with hers, into which he gazed with a look so sombre that it did not suggest any notion of a lover. "Things are going very wrong, and the place suits me as little as it does you."

"Then why do you stay?" cried Stasie, imagining that his state of mind might be due to his affection for his cousin.

"Because, though ill at ease here, I should be miserable away." Then after a short pause he added, in a low tone, almost dreading to venture so bold an opening lest he should startle or repel her—"Sefton Park is the world to me ; I *cannot* leave it."

"Good heavens!" thought Stasie, in some

mental excitement, "is he going to make a confidante of *me*?   I would rather not.   How nice
he is, and how unfortunate!"   Aloud she said,
with some confusion and a vivid blush—"Yet,
don't you think it would be better to go, even if
it were hard to break away?   At least it seems
so to me."

"Does it?" returned Brooke, much struck by
her words, and feeling his heart sink within him.
"Nevertheless I cannot go; a sense of duty,
which I must not explain, keeps me here, as well
as strong inclination.   But I shall not forget
your advice."

"Advice—oh! I do not presume to offer advice to you, who are so much older and wiser
than I am; but there are some things in which
a sort of instinct directs even a mere schoolgirl
like myself."

"And your instinct is against me," cried
Brooke, with a spasm of despair such as he never
dreamed any woman's words would have brought
him.

"Against you! Oh no; *I* am not against
you.   I, if you will let me say so," said Stasie,
who, when consulted or soothed, was humility

itself—" I feel with you and for you, and am
only grieved to think you are unhappy in any
way ; but I do think it would be wiser to go
away." " I suppose he thinks it his duty as a
relation to stop and look after Mrs. Harding," she
thought, " but it is no use, and she is getting on
better."

"Forgive me if I differ from you : I may be
of use. I—I cannot explain to you now ; but
from no personal consideration, no selfish hopes,
I am resolved to remain."

"You know best," said Stasie, a little bewildered ; and there was an embarrassing pause,
mercifully broken by the entrance of Miss
Stretton, fresh and cold from her evening drive.
She was quite *empressée* in her greeting of Dr.
Brooke, but anxious to get away to her toilette.
" Mr. Harding is so particular as to punctuality,
you know, my dear," she explained to her niece ;
so Brooke took the hint and his leave.

But the conversation she had had with him
dwelt long and vividly in Stasie's mind. She
could not have believed that a man like Brooke,
who had impressed upon her the idea of a will
too firm, a temperament too coldly composed, to

be moved by anything short of a moral earthquake, would have been so shaken, so emotional, as he had proved himself during that intensely interesting interview. That Dr. Brooke should have attempted to confide in her was too wonderful.

After all—though, of course, it was not right to love a married woman so very much—she half envied her friend the possession of a heart so true, so disinterested. But that Mrs. Harding should ever give him a warmer thought than what of right belonged to a kind, sympathetic, pleasant kinsman, she never for an instant believed.

"Ah ! how good Mrs. Harding is ! I fear that in her place I should not be so good. Only for the children, they are the great stay."

CHAPTER VI.

THIS conversation produced a profound impression upon Brooke. He could not shake it off. For some hours it filled him with despair.

He sat down to dinner with his host. He listened to his cheerful talk without hearing one word he said while he watched the blue curls of smoke from his cigar and repeated over and over again Stasie's mysterious words—"Had you not better go?" Was there then no hope for him? If so, there was little for her.

Was ever man so cruelly hampered? Was ever knowledge so horribly neutralised? He felt a contempt for himself, for his own impotence. But what could he do? If he attacked either Bhoodhoo or Kharapet, the only result would be a breach, which would make him look like a fool, and deprive him of the only chance to save Stasie. In the present stage of affairs Kharapet might defy suspicion and inquiry. He knew well how the action of such a poison as he feared could be so timed as to close the drama at any moment. No! he must not let Kharapet have the smallest inkling that he was watched and suspected. Here was a position trying and difficult enough, but when Stasie, with sweet yet hesitating honesty that made his heart ache, warned him off the premises as it were, the last ingredient was added to the sea of perplexity in which he felt himself tossed to and fro.

Brooke was by nature a proud, masterful man, only preserved from an over-tendency to dominate by shrewd common-sense and a certain amount of sympathy, qualities which made him at once liked and respected by his fellows; but that he had so soft a heart had never been revealed to him till he knew Stasie Verner, and the sense of danger to her—danger known only to himself—from which he only could save her, fanned his liking into an intense flame.

" If I could get that fellow out to drive with me," he thought of Kharapet, " I would break his neck as unhesitatingly as I would shoot a mad dog or any noxious beast, but I must speak him

fair—I must not let him suppose I doubt him.
And Stasie herself? What a conceited ass I was
to imagine, as I did, that, on the whole, she was
disposed to love me!" Then he began to ponder
on her words—her manner. There was something
in the latter he could not quite understand. She
hesitated to pronounce his sentence of banishment,
but there was none of the shrinking embarrassment that might be expected from a sensitive,
warm-hearted girl fencing off the first approach
to a declaration. Was there any misunderstanding on his part? Could he, in the strong emotion
of the moment, have mistaken her meaning? He
would at any rate see her to-morrow on his way
to consult with Mrs. Harding, whom he would take
partially into his confidence, and endeavour to
recover his lost ground of friendly understanding
—*if* he had lost it.

One pin's point of hope he had gathered from
their conversation; Stasie's imagination could be
touched and alarmed, and she was a little uneasy
at her own sensations. This might help him.
But what a destiny for Stasie if driven only by
fear of death to take refuge in his arms!

"Pooh! I am growing womanish and hysterical," thought Brooke, rallying his forces ; "I must keep cool and resolute : I will make my way out of this cursed deadlock, and save her too, if I have to kill those two infernal plotters with my own hand." "I say, Robinson," he exclaimed, throwing the end of his cigar into the fire, "I have rather a headache, and I am too stupid for companionship, so I will be off to bed."

. . . . .

As early as politeness permitted, Brooke sallied forth next day to call on his cousin. He had watched from his window till he saw Mr. Harding pass at a rapid pace to catch the nine o'clock train, which carried the bread-winners of Sefton Park cityward to their daily toil, and with some difficulty kept quiet for an hour or more with the help of a weed and the morning papers, till he thought he might venture to present himself.

He walked slowly up the road. Slackening his pace as he neared Limeville, he was devoured with the desire to understand fully what Stasie meant when she told him " he had better go." He was painfully anxious to regain the friendly footing he feared had been endangered, and he began to confess to himself that at all times he would take some trouble to rejoice his eyes with the sight of her. On reaching the gate, he saw it stood half open, and at the sound of his footsteps Pearl flew out bounding and barking the wildest welcome. Brooke stooped to caress the dog. "You must not wander away and loose yourself, you little beggar! you are much too precious." He lifted the dog as he spoke, intending to put him inside the gate and close it; but while he stroked the little creature, Stasie came quickly out of the house as though in chase of her favourite.

"Ah, Dr. Brooke!" she exclaimed, pausing as she reached the road; "you have caught that naughty little dog—he is always trying to run away." She looked bright, sunny, and, unless he was stupidly conceited, glad to see him.

"Here is the little culprit safe and sound, Miss Verner. Who is your gatekeeper? You should insist on its being shut, or Master Pearl will break bounds on every occasion."

"I have no such important functionary," said Stasie, laughing; "but I will ask Bhoodhoo to see it is kept closed; he is so thoughtful. Come, Pearl, you must stay at home to-day, and be brushed and made pretty, for your old master is coming to see you."

"Has Pearson returned?" asked Brooke quickly, as he followed Stasie into the pleasure-ground.

"Yes. He sent Aunt Clem a brace of partridge last night, and a note saying he would ride over to-day. I shall be glad to hear about poor dear Lady Pearson and his brother."

Brooke was silent for a minute or two, and Stasie, the gate being shut, set down Pearl, and began to gather some of the few autumnal flowers still blooming.

"Why haven't you a shawl or something to wrap round you?" said Brooke abruptly. "The air is crisp."

"I do not need it. I am going in immediately."

"Is it permitted to ask how you slept?" he continued with a smile.

"Yes," returned Stasie; "that is a common civility. I slept better than usual, and am like a giant refreshed."

"Good. I am rejoiced to hear it. Now, I will venture another question; answer me truly."

His deep-set eyes grew so earnest, so imploring, that they fascinated hers, " Will it annoy or offend you if I stay on here ? "

" Annoy me ? " cried Stasie, surprised, but not embarrassed ; " no, certainly not. Why should it ? "

" I do not know ; only I gathered from your words yesterday that it would be unwise of me to stay."

" Oh, yes ! I remember," she said, recalling their conversation, and colouring vividly. " I am afraid I was rather presumptuous, but "— breaking off abruptly—" you know best. Let us say no more about it. How could you imagine your staying here would annoy *me* ? "

Brooke was silent, seeking in vain for a solution of her puzzling remarks. Could it be that her fancy was disordered by the action of the poison he believed had been given her ? At all events, she did not wish him to go. What could she have meant ? " Then I shall certainly remain," said he at length. " And, tell me, have you been eating helwa since ? "

" No," returned Stasie, raising her eyes smilingly to his, " I am quite willing to take care of myself, but I hide it away not to offend Bhoodhoo, who is so pleased to think I like it."

"Quite right," said Brooke eagerly. "Give it to me when you want to get rid of it. See if Pearl will eat it."

"I have tried him, but he will not."

"I am going to Mrs. Harding's. I am going to suggest her consulting Filmer about you, Miss Verner. Promise me not to resist her advice."

"I will not," said Stasie thoughtfully. "But, Dr. Brooke, tell Mrs. Harding to speak first to Aunt Clem. She likes to be first in everything, and she is very good to me."

"And you to her, I am sure. I will remember your hint. So good-bye for the present."

He raised his hat, and walked away up the road. Stasie continued to search for and gather what blossoms were left, while she thought somewhat eagerly of the change she had suddenly become aware of in Dr. Brooke. For some reason or other he was deeply, unmistakably anxious about herself. His manner, too, had lost its calm superiority. There was a something less assured, something curiously pleading, in his eyes, his voice, that conveyed to her a subtile sense of her own importance. Why was it so? On account of her close intimacy with Mrs. Harding? It must be. Stasie had carefully ruled her thoughts, her imagination, had resisted all temptation to let either dwell on Brooke, but to-day she could not. She compared him mentally to the various brilliant young men she had met while staying with Lady Pearson. How immeasurably superior he was to them all! To her the quiet strength which his tone and aspect expressed was infinitely attractive. He was so equable, so just and broad in his opinions; and although his composure might seem cold, she had a conviction that beneath it was a deep spring of warm sympathy for the few he loved. Then, to her inexperience, he seemed to know everything. Why, it was wonderful that he should take as much interest as he did in a mere half-instructed girl like herself, especially as at first she must have seemed but too ready to worry him with her questions and her company. For though full of high and gallant spirit, Stasie had a genuinely humble opinion of herself, and shrunk from the idea of thrusting herself forward, as she would from a blow. Was Dr. Brooke in love with his cousin, as Aunt Clem thought? It was impossible to say!

Meanwhile Brooke went on a little more at ease, from Stasie's frank assurance. He found Mrs. Harding busy over her house accounts, and alone.

" Don't let me disturb you," he said. " I will go smoke my cigar under the lime-trees. Send for me when you can spare a few minutes; I want to talk with you."

It was a crisp gray morning, and as Brooke loitered to and fro in a little grove of limes which sheltered one end of the house, his courage and composure seemed to return. If Stasie was quite willing he should stay, he must have entirely misunderstood her. His chief aim now must be to impress his own feelings upon her, to convey to her his hope, to win her and save her, and join to his own that young buoyant life, that tender, generous heart. What a vista of delight!

Here a servant summoned him to Mrs. Harding's presence. After exchanging a few commonplaces, she asked—

" What did you want to talk to me about, Jim?"

He paused an instant, and then determined to be quite confidential up to the limit of the dreadful secret of his real trouble. He said in a quiet steady voice, " I am uneasy about Stasie Verner, Livy."

" Indeed ! " with keenly-aroused attention. " Why, Jim ? "

" Because I see a return of those symptoms which so alarmed us before. Believe me, she ought to have advice—the advice of a first-rate man."

" You alarm me. What do you think is the matter with her ? "

" I could not tell without going more deeply into the question than she would permit. Something perhaps of the nature of heart disease, which will not be incurable if it be not hereditary. Kharapet says her mother died of heart disease. "

" I do not think she did. I perfectly remember old Mr. Kharapet describing her wasting away from continued attacks of fever, to which she finally succumbed. No ; she did not die of heart disease."

" Why does Kharapet assert it then ? "

"He may have heard she did! He can have no motive. Somehow, I always search for 'motives' with Mr. Kharapet."

"Well, Livy, I want you to persuade Miss Verner to go to my friend Filmer. He is a profound pathologist, and if any one can do her good, *he* can; but get the aunt to view the matter in its true light, as of the last importance. I tell you, that sweet bright girl may slip through our fingers before we know where we are."

There was suppressed emotion in his voice. Mrs. Harding looked up surprised.

"You are very deeply interested in Stasie, Jim."

"I am; Livy, she is everything to me!"

"I hardly expected this," returned Mrs. Harding thoughtfully; "there is so little of a lover in your style and manner; but I am very, very glad. I love Stasie; and if any man can stand the trials and temptations of matrimony, I *fancy* you can. But, oh! Jim, be good and kind to her."

"My dear cousin! do you think there is the faintest hope for me?" very eagerly.

" I cannot tell—indeed I cannot; but if I could I would not."

" Why ? "

" Because it would be treachery. I really think Stasie is perfectly fancy free. Try, oh try, to win her ! "

" I need no urging ! but I fear ——," he paused, and, rising, began to pace the room. " That young Pearson has returned," he resumed.

" Has he ? I do not think Stasie would ever care for him—she feels herself stronger than he is."

" He is a nice young fellow ; but *he* could not save her ! " said Brooke, as if to himself.

" How do you mean, Jim ? "

" Nothing. If I were to succeed with Miss Verner, I suppose I should encounter a tremendous opposition from Kharapet and your husband, and, through them, from the guardian ? "

" From Kharapet, yes ; but I am not so sure about Mr. Harding. I am certain he dislikes Kharapet, but does not like to show it. Still, in time you could get over all that."

" Ay, time—and time is so infinitely precious."

" But, Jim, you are quite young yet !—not

two years older than I am! You need not be in such a violent hurry."

"I am though, Livy; in a most violent hurry."

"I should have thought you a more reasonable man," said Mrs. Harding, with a smile.

"In this matter I am utterly unreasonable," exclaimed Brooke, throwing himself into his chair again, "and you must be my friend—you must help me, Livy! I do not say it from self-conceit; but I sincerely believe it will be best for Stasie Verner to marry me. If she is heart-whole I think there is a good chance for me. I do not think I should be attracted to her as I am if she did not feel a certain sympathy for me!"

"Perhaps so; but, Jim, how many men have lavished the warmest affection on women who did not care a straw for them!"

"True; but ours—mine is no ordinary case;" this impetuously, then in an altered tone, "By Jove! I am only saying what every blockhead thinks when he first falls in love. Yet there *is* something more, but I cannot tell you."

"You are quite mysterious," said Mrs. Harding, smiling. "I must not flatter you by admitting there is anything out of the common in your case, except that you are very far gone, much farther than I thought."

" I could hardly be in a deeper depth," returned Brooke; " and I claim your friendly aid."

" So far as I can, I will gladly help you, Jim ; but I do not think you have much opposition to fear, except from Hormuz Kharapet."

" Has he still any hopes of success with Miss Verner ? " asked Brooke.

" No ; that is, he seems formally and openly to have resigned that project, but Heaven only knows what his real views are. Of one thing I am sure he will oppose her marriage with any one. He would neither like to give an account of his stewardship nor give up the manipulation of her money until compelled by her being of age."

" Three years," murmured Brooke, " and in that time what infinite evil might be wrought ! "

" I should be very glad indeed if you and Stasie were to marry soon. She is terribly isolated, and I should like as much of her money as possible to be saved."

" So should I," returned Brooke, " for every reason, though I would gladly marry her to-morrow if she had not a rap, imprudent though it would be."

"*I* believe you, Jim, but many would not. Well, count on me ; so far as a third person can help, I will."

" The first thing to be done," said Brooke, rousing himself from a fit of thought, " is to induce Miss Stretton to take her niece to Filmer. Frequent short changes of scene would be useful. Not a family exodus, you understand, just by herself."

After some further discussion it was agreed that Mrs. Harding should attack Miss Stretton that very day, and Brooke accepted a commission to go up to town and change a book in which both Stasie and her friend were deeply interested, for the second and third volumes, which would give him an excuse for presenting himself at Limeville in the afternoon, where Mrs. Harding promised to meet him and observe what effect Mr. Pearson's visit appeared to produce.

.   .   .   .   .

It was not difficult to deal with Miss Stretton.

She was keenly alive to the importance of Stasie's health, and sincerely anxious to see it completely re-established. Still she evidently would not positively agree to anything till she had consulted Kharapet. He made his appearance a couple of days later, very opportunely, as he often did when any matter of importance was under consideration—so often that Mrs. Harding suspected Aunt Clem of daily private communication with him.

The influence of the Syrian over her was enormous, her present and future alike depended on him, she thought, and as his personal flattery grew less fine in quality as well as quantity, a little wholesome fear began to leaven her strong liking and admiration of the gentle Hormuz.

Stasie's wrath was often raised by the tremendous fuss made by her aunt respecting Mr. Kharapet's comforts and Mr. Kharapet's favourite dishes, which were, as Mary the housemaid remarked, " a goodish few, and wasn't it a mercy that nice obliging man Bhoodhoo was there to cook them ? Such a mixing and a stewing and a simmering Susan never could manage ! but bless you, he cares for nothing but to muddle among his saucepans all day long."

Whatever Kharapet's needs, however, they were elaborately supplied; and Stasie declared she felt as nothing and nobody in the house, when Kharapet was there.

On the present occasion he was peculiarly amiable, and quite tender in his solicitude for Stasie.

He thought her not looking at all well, and heartily agreed in Mrs. Harding's opinion that the advice of a first-rate physician should be sought. Why not Sir Harcourt Filmer? He himself would have suggested the famous Dr. Carus, who always attended my Lord Saintsbury, but it was really of no importance which of these eminent men were employed.

Stasie made no objection. She had been unusually quiet—even languid for the last few days—averse to take long walks, and impervious to Van Pearson's compliments and sallies. She felt impatient to throw off this oppression, and was full of hope for the results of consulting a new and a great doctor.

Brooke had made up his mind to keep as much as possible out of Kharapet's way; their meeting would do no good, and the strain on his (Brooke's) self-control was too great when in the presence of a man whom he suspected of such treachery.

He ascertained, however, from Mrs. Harding the day fixed upon for Stasie's visit to Sir Harcourt Filmer, and wrote a private note re-commending her to his special attention, and begging for a personal interview subsequently.

Then he eagerly waited the result.

The afternoon on which Stasie and Miss Stretton returned after seeing the great doctor, Brooke could not refrain from loitering about the station at the time the train was due. Here to his great relief he was joined by Mrs. Harding, whose evening ramble with the children brought her that way.

She dismissed them and sat down with him on a bench outside, where from the elevated road-way there was a pretty view over the Sefton woods.

" Their train is overdue," said Brooke, looking at his watch for the second time, after a pause in their intermittent talk.

" And you are over anxious ! You are really looking ill yourself, Jim, which alarms me, not for you, but for Stasie."

He made no reply. As she spoke the expected train came round a bend of the line, and steamed rapidly into the station, overshooting the platform.

Brooke hastened to assist Miss Stretton, who went on at once to Mrs. Harding, with whom she entered into animated conversation. Stasie waited to collect some parcels, without which no lady ever returned from London to Sefton Park, and then gave Brooke her hand as she descended.

She looked pale and preoccupied, and Brooke, as his questioning eyes dwelt upon her, imagined he read disappointment in her expression. Her first words were commonplace enough. " Pray ask one of the porters to take these things across and keep them till we send down for them, and there is a small basket in the guard's van."

" I will see to it," and he left her for a moment. When he returned the train had moved on, and Mrs. Harding with Miss Stretton were already crossing the line to the gate of exit.

Stasie was standing quite still, and gazing away over the gently-rising upland with its variegated greens and browns, crowned by woods which were in their last glories of autumnal colouring; there was a sad wistful look in her big thoughtful eyes. Brooke thought they glittered suspiciously, as if full of unshed tears. Was it possible that she had drawn some discouraging impression from her interview with Filmer. Dare he hope that his old master's wide knowledge and professional acumen had detected something of the truth?

"Miss Stretton has gone on," he said.

"Oh, yes; I am coming," said Stasie in a dreamy voice, and began to follow slowly.

Brooke was burning to question her, yet hesitated how to begin. After a few steps in silence, Stasie exclaimed, "I am *so* tired."

"Are you?" cried Brooke; "would you like to sit down here, while I get the pony and trap from the railway inn for you?"

"Oh, no thank you; that would be much ado about nothing," she returned with a smile, having apparently quite recovered any unusual emotion she might have felt.

"Then walk slowly, and tell me—what do you think of Filmer?"

"I am not sure; I thought him rather grumpy at first. But, oh, what an eye he has! he looks through one."

"Doctors are bound to study a patient's physiognomy."

"I suppose so; *you* have something of that piercingness yourself; and when you are a great doctor it will be much worse—or better," said Stasie in her natural, impulsive way.

"Am I to be a great doctor, Miss Verner?"

"Yes, I fancy you *will* be,"—a pause.

"And were you satisfied with your interview?" asked Brooke; he listened eagerly for her reply, which did not come for a second or two.

"No," she said at length softly, with a touch of sadness in her voice, "not at all, rather disappointed. I did so hope for some quite new remedy, some little bit of information about myself, and he just said nothing more than poor old Mr. Hunter did; he talked of debility, and slight derangement of digestion, and gave me a prescription. We had it made up, and I believe it is just the same as Dr. Hunter gave me."

"Indeed! you must remember that doctors

never tell their patients much about themselves."

"That may be, but I am quite sure Sir Harcourt Filmer does not think there is much the
matter with me. I fancied he was vexed at
having his time taken up with such a mere
nothing as my complaints, and I described my
sensations *so* badly ! "

" But is it not encouraging to find he thinks
there is so little the matter with you ? "

" No," said Stasie, " for "—she hesitated, and
then burst out with irrepressible confidence—" I
am *not* well; I can't tell you how I feel ! But
this world is so lovely, and life so delightful, I
want to enjoy it ! I want to feel my own old
self again. Why, it used to be delicious even to
wake up in the morning and feel I was alive—
oh, how alive."

" You *shall* feel it again," said Brooke emphatically, in a tone that struck to Stasie's heart.
He was deeply moved. If he dared speak out to
her? But the danger of it ! Suppose she were
averse to him in the character of a lover, would
it not cut her off from all the chances of escape
which her frank confidence in him offered.

" You think I shall ! ah, I hope so ! "

" Miss Verner, if this prescription fails, will you let *me* have my innings?"

" We will see."

" Did Filmer advise change of air ? "

" Not very strongly, but Aunt Clem rather caught at the idea, and has been planning an exodus of the whole household to Torquay or Bournemouth all the way back."

" That won't do ! If you go you must go alone," said Brooke with decision.

Stasie looked at him with some surprise, and opened her lips to reply, when Miss Stretton turned back suddenly, and joined in the conversation, to assure Brooke of her great satisfaction in finding that Sir Harcourt Filmer entirely agreed with " that dear good Dr. Hunter in whom I have the greatest confidence," etc.

.   .   .   .   .

Brooke was, on the whole, more hopeful after this conversation with Stasie. If he could but win her confidence and steal into her regard without startling her into an attitude of self-defence, there was hope still.

That evening's post brought Brooke a note

from Filmer, appointing the next day but one for the interview he had asked.

"Now for a bold stroke to secure my only chance of help. If I can convince Filmer, all may yet go well."

CHAPTER VII.

WITH anxious punctuality Brooke reached Harley
Street a few minutes before the hour appointed
by the great doctor.

Sir Harcourt Filmer, however, was still engaged,
the servant informed him; and Brooke accord-
ingly composed himself to bide his time as best
he could in the dreary waiting-room, where so
many hearts had fluttered with hesitating hope,
or sunk in darkest doubt.

He thought over again all he intended to lay
before his former master, striving to reduce his
ideas into the smallest and most compact form,
consistent with clearness, that he might not
occupy too many of the minutes, which were
literally worth their weight in gold.

He was still marshalling his few facts, and the
inferences he had deduced from them, when a

door opposite opened, and the well-known physician stood on the threshold.

"Ah! you are there, are you? Come in! Come and have some luncheon. We can talk while eating, and I shall not lose time."

He led the way through the consulting-room to a very comfortable study, where a coal and wood fire glowed in a grate of the newest and most improved fashion, and a table was laid for two.

The doctor rang sharply, and his summons was quickly responded to by a servant, who brought in the expected luncheon.

"That will do," said Sir Harcourt, as soon as they were seated. "Put the bell by me, and you need not wait. What will you take, Brooke?"

"I do not want anything; if you will let me talk while you eat I should much prefer it."

"Very well. At least take a glass of wine."

"Presently, thank you."

"And now, what is it that disturbs you about the girl you sent me? I have just looked at my notes, and there is not much the matter with her."

" You think not ? I am very uneasy on her account."

" I fancy she is a little out of sorts. In short, in the nervous, restless, depressed condition very common with young girls before they have attained their full strength. Do you know if any of her people had heart disease ? I rather think her heart may be a little weak. The other symptoms — sleeplessness, nausea, etc., can be accounted for in various ways, none of them alarming. I have given her a few drops of tincture digitalis in combination with valerian and iron."

" You evidently see nothing out of the common in her case ? "

" Nothing whatever ; and I am surprised that you alarm yourself, but I suppose you have had less to do with feminine ailments and fancies (which are often synonymous terms), than I have. I assure you, half the practice in London is made up of just such nondescript maladies as your young friend's. She is a fine girl, though ! She ought not to be ill."

"She was in perfect, almost ideal, health when I first met her about six months ago," said Brooke. "I had been away for some time, and on my return

I found her greatly changed, so·much so that I ventured to speak to the local man who attended her—a very sensible, ordinary practitioner. He took the same view of the case as you do. I, for special reasons, induced him to order change of air. The effect was wonderful; but circumstances occurred which obliged her to come back too soon, then all the symptoms reappeared even worse than before. I have inquired as far as I could as to the cause of her mother's death. Her aunt says it was repeated fever, while Kharapet, a Syrian, brother of her late stepfather, and one of his executors, declares he always understood that the mother died of heart disease.

"Ah!" said Sir Harcourt.

"I do not believe him, and the aunt stoutly denies it."

"Hum! The aunt is that elderly chatterbox that came with her? She has not as much brains as you could stick on the point of a needle!"

"Just the woman to be made a tool of," said Brooke thoughtfully.

"Very likely," returned Sir Harcourt.

"You consider then that there is no cause for

uneasiness—I mean Miss Verner's friends need not be anxious?"

"No, certainly not. The worst symptom is her sleeplessness, but that will pass as her general health improves."

"*If* it improves," said Brooke very emphatically.

"What is the matter? I say, Brooke, are you sweet on the young lady? If so, why, your judgment may not be very sound."

"At any rate," returned Brooke, "I am very deeply interested in her, because I have a theory which I beg you to consider a professional secret."

"Out with it then! We doctors are accustomed to queer corners behind the smooth surface of society."

"I will be as brief as possible," returned Brooke. "This girl, Miss Verner, is the step-daughter of the late British Consul at Mardīn. The old man was much attached to her, and left her all his money—a considerable sum. He named as executors, Mr. Harding a merchant of some standing, and his own younger brother, Hormuz Kharapet, a protégé of Percy Wyatt's and some of the Exeter Hall saints."

"I have met him," ejaculated Sir Harcourt Filmer.

"Well," continued Brooke, "this Kharapet has devoted himself to Miss Verner. He is or was madly in love with her. She has rejected him,—that is, I am almost sure she has,—but he still hangs about her. She lives a short way out of town with her aunt, who came here with her, and who has the firmest faith in Kharapet. The household consists of a ladies' maid, another female servant, and a coloured man, a cook, recommended by Kharapet."

"What does all this lead to?" asked Sir Harcourt, as Brooke paused suddenly, struck by the difficulty of impressing his hearer with his own convictions.

"For more than two months," resumed Brooke, "Miss Verner's health has been failing. She goes away for a fortnight—all her bad symptoms vanish. She returns, and they re-appear. This Eastern is perpetually at the house. A girl like Miss Verner—of a physique so fine, with every indication of splendid health —ought not to break down in this way without an accident—an illness—a visible cause."

"These things are hard to account for without a very thorough knowledge of the patient's circumstances. What are you driving at, Brooke?"

"Should Stasie Verner die under age her property goes to Kharapet. Had she married him he would have had a lovely wife and a good fortune. He is not the man to lose both. He is slowly removing the obstacle to his greed—the woman who denied him."

"My dear sir!" cried the physician, opening his eyes, "you are positively dramatic. Would you have me believe it is a case of poisoning?"

"I believe it is."

"Come, come, Brooke! You must have lost your head; just think of the certain detection which would follow such an attempt! How could a system of secret poisoning go on where a number of people are living in the same house, eating the same food, drinking the same beverages? others would be affected. No one would be mad enough to venture on so daring a piece of villainy!"

"Nevertheless he *is* venturing it, I am fully convinced. When first my suspicions were

roused, I made Stasie give me some of the sweetmeats that cook of hers makes, and——"

"Ha! you analysed them," exclaimed Sir
Harcourt eagerly.

"No; analysis is most difficult with the class
of poisons I suspect Kharapet uses. No; I ate
them myself."

"The deuce, you did! and what then? You
are alive to tell the tale."

"Yes; I was pretty sure the dose would not
be strong enough to do *me* much harm; but it
was not without effect. I felt something of the
fever, the nausea, the palpitation that are playing
the mischief with that sweet, unoffending girl,
and which will end in her death if Kharapet's
doings are not put a stop to."

"That's rather curious," said Sir Harcourt
thoughtfully; "but you are evidently imagina-
tive—you might have fancied these symptoms.
The correct plan would have been to analyse."

"I will have a piece of the helwa analysed by
some good chemist, but I question if it will be of
much avail."

"My dear fellow, I am sorry you have allowed
yourself to be overmastered by a fixed idea. Be

the temptation what it may, you will never persuade me that a man like this Kharapet (I sat next him at dinner at Lady Kilconquhar's, and he seemed rather a superior man), a man well received in good society—in all respects a gentleman; that such a man would run the risk of attempting the crime you suppose—for what? to possess himself of a comparatively small fortune (the young lady is not a millionaire, is she?), and to revenge himself on a girl who had refused him! Why, few men care enough about yes or no in such a matter—an Oriental least of all! You must remember how nearly impossible it is to obliterate the traces of poison, and, I should say, quite impossible to administer it to one member of a family who has no need to take any especial medicine or keep to a particular diet without injuring the rest more or less. This would involve immediate suspicion."

" I see how the circumstances must appear to you, yet my impression is still the same," said Brooke, with some eagerness, though he strove hard to be cool. " I should have taken the same view had I not seen some curious cases of poisoning in India, did I not know there is a poison used by those scoundrels, the Thugs, since they abandoned the sacred noose, which our best analysts could not detect, so rapidly is it absorbed and eliminated when given in small and repeated doses, as is, I believe, their plan."

" But this Kharapet is a Christian—a Syrian. He may be as ignorant of this poison as I am," exclaimed Sir Harcourt.

" He has lived much in Rajpootana and other native states, where the deadly *Datura stramonium* grows on the roadsides and offers easy means to put away an enemy or slay a stranger to propitiate their sanguinary goddess."

" Still, I doubt if Kharapet would attempt such a crime, or, indeed, that he could carry it out. What is there in this man's character or antecedents which leads you to suspect him?"

" I know nothing of his antecedents," returned Brooke, " nor do I know anything against his character ; but I confess I have disliked and distrusted him from the first."

" Ah! just so! There, I suspect, lies the key to the riddle. You must not let prejudice or imagination run away with you. Cool sound judgment is the most essential quality in a medical man. Put these crotchets out of your head; if you take action under their influence they will lead you into a mess that will be anything but advantageous to your future career. It is not like what I remember of you, to be led away by fancy. There is some under current of which I know nothing. If I were you, and so deeply interested in the young lady, I should just take her under my own care altogether, especially as she has the wherewithal; only, I should like a sounder condition of health in a wife. Send her to me in a fortnight; I feel sure I shall find her greatly improved."

"Certainly, she shall have the benefit of your advice; but my doubts and suspicions are not in the slightest degree changed by your natural and sensible observations. I must do the best I can unassisted."

.   .   .   .   .

This interview produced a terribly depressing effect on Brooke; it proved to him the enormous barrier which habit and custom raises against the admission of a new idea. Filmer was a learned and enlightened man, broad-minded in the best sense of the word; yet a life passed among proprieties, and in a society from which the "shocking" was carefully excluded, made it impossible for him to believe that such a tragedy as Brooke had suggested was being enacted within a twenty-four mile radius of St. Martin's-le-Grand. Had it been a piece of legal or stock-broking chicanery, or the design of a spiteful servant, or the proposed crime of some vulgar ruffian, Sir Harcourt might have lent a ready ear and a helping hand; but that a smooth-spoken well-mannered man, admitted into some of the best houses in town—a man who, from his position and education, must be aware of the value of character—should risk all his advantages for the sake of melodramatic revenge and preposterous greed, was too much opposed to English common-sense, too much like the plot of a second-rate French novel, to be credited by a Briton cradled in conventionality for so many years, as the great doctor had been.

Brooke, as he walked away from the house, felt half angry with himself for not having foreseen this. Twenty years ago, when Filmer was a young struggling man, he would have taken in the idea more readily; " as it is, prosperity has so padded the walls of life's cell for him, he forgets that beneath the cushions are rugged stones, rude angles, rusted iron clamps. Now I must act alone and unaided."

He made his way to his club, and finding one or two acquaintances there who were passing through town, tried to change the current of his thoughts by talk on various ordinary topics, thus seeking relief for an hour or two, that he might return with fresh vigour to the all-important question of his future line of conduct.

Meanwhile Stasie Verner's head and heart were much occupied by conjecture as to what could be the real meaning of her last conversations with Brooke. At first she never doubted that when he avowed, in an impulsive, irrepressible way, that he was miserable at Sefton Park, yet could not leave it, and that it was the world to him, that he was on the point of confessing his affection for Mrs. Harding; yet what could be more improbable than that a grave, self-possessed man like Brooke, a man so much her superior in age as well as everything else, should make a confidante of her? It was, no doubt, an involuntary expression of feeling of which he was scarce conscious; but if so, how unhappy he must be, and how Stasie longed to comfort him! But it would be better for him to go; there was no good in staying. As to Mrs. Harding, no one in the world could come between her and her children; and no doubt Dr. Brooke was well aware of this, or a man of his principles (as she supposed) would go fast enough. But all these conclusions were upset by his last words on this delicate topic. When he absolutely asked her leave to remain where he was, there could be no doubt of his being truly and deeply in earnest. She seemed still to see the intense questioning of his dark eyes. The relieved look that came into them when she exclaimed naturally that his re-maining could not annoy her—what could he mean? Surely her opinion or permission could have little value in his eyes. Could he possibly be interested in herself? Her heart beat at the thought; but instinctively she turned from it. She was tacitly aware—tacitly even in her most candid self-communing—that the idea was too delightful, too flattering, to be looked at, lest it should haunt and master her.

After all, if Dr. Brooke was interested in her,

it was probably as " a case." He certainly
thought her very unwell ; he was anxious about
her, in that she did not deceive herself, and he
was clever, deep-seeing, quite beyond the average
of doctors. This conviction made her not so much
uneasy as depressed about herself; she never
could describe the many curious and unpleasant
sensations which from time to time disturbed
her. The sudden beatings of the heart that came
and went so mysteriously, the curious hallucina-
tions that flitted through her brain : for sometimes she could have sworn she saw Pearl, or a
wild black cat that often visited the garden, come
into the room, though she knew both door and
window were shut ; she had even risen from her
seat to look for the creature she imagined. Such
things as these she was ashamed to tell. She
blamed herself for such fancies ; yet the conviction grew on her that no one save Dr. Brooke
knew how ill she really was. Still she could not
conquer her reluctance to consult him ; and a
curious nervous dread of she did not know
what, began to fasten upon her from the day
Sir Harcourt Filmer made so light of her complaints.

In such a condition of mind Mr. Pearson's visits were a most agreeable means of escaping from herself, and Mrs. Harding's warning was partially forgotten. Moreover, Aunt Clem was so visibly vexed at his coming that Stasie felt bound to receive him with cordiality.

"What is the reason I don't get on with your aunt?" he asked confidentially, one wet afternoon two or three days after Brooke's interview with Sir Harcourt Filmer, as he was sitting beside Stasie's work-table. He had ridden over in spite of wind and weather, and had been very warmly welcomed by Stasie; soon after his arrival Aunt Clem had been summoned out of the room by the arrival of "Mr. Kharapet, who is very wet,'m, and must change his things before he comes into the drawing-room," the servant announced. Of course, Miss Stretton fussed away to see to that gentleman's comfort.

"Oh! you get on with her very well," said Stasie carelessly.

"Not a bit of it. I wish you would give me the 'tip,' Miss Verner; I want to make friends with her. In general, elderly ladies are deuced fond of me; I assure you they are."

"I am afraid you think every one is fond of you, Mr. Pearson."

"I wish *every* one was fond of me," cried the young man with emphasis; "but I am afraid it is just those I like best that care least for me."

"I imagine that is often the case," returned Stasie dreamily as she played with Pearl's ears.

"By Jove, Miss Verner, you have such a way of shutting a fellow up."

"I don't want to shut you up," said Stasie, turning a pair of beautiful wondering eyes upon him. "I want you to talk, for I am very dull—tell me about Lady Pearson?"

"Oh, my mother is better; you know she has been quite worn out nursing Frank; but he is doing very well, and she gets more rest. She sent her love to you. She hopes, as soon as my brother is all right, you'll come and stay with her. Though it's not the season, there is a good deal of fun to be had in London towards the end of November. Any place would be better than this hole; why, even you, and I am sure you have no end of pluck, you can't stand it—you looked twice as bright at Southsea."

"You don't think me looking ill, do you?"

cried Stasie, starting up and going to look at herself in the glass with undisguised interest; " why, you are as bad as Dr. Brooke."

" Brooke ! Oh, he couldn't take a cheerful view of anything. He is going melancholy mad, I believe. Why, he was at my father's two or three times last season, and we all thought him an uncommonly pleasant fellow. I never saw a man so changed."

" What do you think is the reason ? " asked Stasie, with much interest, as she resumed her seat.

" Well, I do not fancy it is far to seek," said the young lancer, with an expressive look, which his companion did not see, as she was busy taking up a dropped stitch in her knitting. " But as to *your* looking ill, I never meant anything of the kind. Ill or well, I—I seldom see any one like you."

Stasie made no reply ; she still looked earnestly at her knitting, but not a shade of consciousness passed over her grave face. Poor Van Pearson felt as if cold water had been poured over him, and would rather have taken a wigging from his Colonel than resumed the subject.

There was an awkward pause; and then, to cover his defeat, Pearson resumed his original topic. " At any rate Kharapet is A.1 with Miss Stretton. Does she always rub him down when he comes in from exercise ? "

" What a funny way of putting it ! " said Stasie, laughing. " She is very fond of him certainly, and he is dreadfully afraid of taking cold, so——"

" He seems afraid of a good many things," interrupted Pearson. " Do you remember the day Pearl snapped at him ? "

" I do indeed. He can't help being nervous, I suppose."

" Nervous ! " repeated Pearson with infinite contempt; " why, he hasn't the courage of a canary. These dark fellows never have."

" I would not say that," replied Stasie. "How calmly Easterns can die. I have heard they do not value life."

" The lives of others, I dare say," cried Pearson. " I do not like them."

" Ah, that is prejudice. It is strange how prejudiced even good-natured people like Mrs. Harding and yourself are about, or rather against Easterns." Mr. Pearson murmured something inarticulate in reply, and then proposed to give Pearl a lesson in begging, in which pastime a quarter of an hour passed merrily, and then, seeing no possible excuse for staying, he rose to take leave.

" It is very good-natured of you to come over to this stupid place," said Stasie unguardedly.

" Good-natured," cried Pearson, colouring ; " good to myself, you mean. Why, if I came as often as I wished, I'd be here every day, only I am afraid you would be tired of me."

" No, I should not," began Stasie ; then, catching sight of such a glow of triumph and joy in his eyes, she hastened to do away with the false impression she had unwittingly created. " That is, if one has a friend—a pleasant friend—one does not easily tire of him or—her." This was brought out with such hesitating confusion that her listener might well be excused for finding encouragement in her broken sentence.

" But, Miss Verner, may I venture to hope I am welcome ? Ah, you must know I should like to be with you all day, and every day of my life ! "

A sense of sudden guilty confusion wrapped

Stasie as if in a burning cloud. She should never have allowed him to get this length. It was terrible to undeceive him—she liked him so much —he was frank and boyish. With a great effort she forced herself to speak. " But that cannot be, you know, Mr. Pearson ; our roads in life will probably be widely apart."

" You *intend* them to be apart, you mean ? "

" I do," said Stasie gravely, and bending her head.

" What an unspeakable idiot I am to have spoken so soon ! " cried Pearson ; " pray, pray forget it ; let us be friends as we were."

" Oh yes, always friends ; but you will forgive me—you will not think me unkind ?—never anything more."

" Never anything more ! you are too unkind —too cruel, Miss Verner ; and I cannot help loving you ! Perhaps I may win you yet—I cannot give up hope ! "

He seized and kissed her hand, and then rushed away, nearly overturning Kharapet, who had paused in the doorway, a spectator of poor Pearson's adieux.

Stasie was greatly moved, and really sorry to

lose the bright young fellow's society, and, as was natural to a girl full of warm feeling, over-estimated considerably the force of the blow she had been obliged to administer. She threw herself on the sofa, and yielded to an hysterical fit of crying—a tendency which she had often to resist, even when there was little or no moving cause.

Kharapet stood looking at her for an instant, his eyes kindling, a tremor stealing through his muscles. He could not imagine what affected Stasie so violently. He stole nearer, and again paused. What if she had quarrelled with this insolent young man? Perhaps in her vexation she might turn to him. Still he hesitated to speak until, with a vague, uneasy sensation that something or some one was near her, she turned and met his eyes.

"Stasie!" he uttered, in a strange, suppressed, imploring way. "You are unhappy; you shed tears! What vexes you? Can I not help, can I not comfort you? What has that young man said or done? How did he dare to kiss your hands?"

"You are really very tiresome, Hormuz," said

Stasie impatiently. She was indignant and a little frightened at his tone. "You have no right to ask."

"I have every right! Tell me, have you sent him away? I thought you loved him, Stasie. If you had, bitter as it would be to me, I should have forwarded your union; if—— Tell me frankly, have you dismissed him because you feared my opposition or Mr. Harding's? Speak, and do not fear; all depends on me. As to Mr. Harding"—he struck his open palms across each other, with that Eastern gesture expressive of nothingness—"I hold him in my hand. Speak, Stasie; do you wish that young man recalled?"

"No, certainly not," returned Stasie, somewhat touched by Kharapet's words. He is very nice and good, but I do not want him back."

"I thought you loved him, Stasie. He is of your own race; you cannot despise him as you do the poor Syrian whose fathers worshipped the true God and His divine Son, when *yours* were heathens."

"I do not despise you, Hormuz! How have I ever shown it? I am grateful to you for all your kindness, and——"

"Then, if you do not love him," interrupted Kharapet, drawing closer to her, "whom do you love? Is your heart, indeed, still empty? Ah, Stasie! is there then still a chance for me? You do not know how I have suffered and languished for you! You do not know," closing his eyes and stretching out his arms towards her for a moment, and then dropping them to his side, "you do not know from what misery your love would save me, from what you would save yourself, if—if only you would be mine."

"Well, but I cannot; you know I cannot," cried Stasie, infinitely annoyed by this return to the old conflict between them. "Can I not exist without being in love? I wish you would not worry yourself and me. We had grown quite comfortable and friendly; why will you begin it all over again? There is no accounting for one's fancies or feelings. You will find many charming girls willing enough to marry you, and I shall always like you as——"

"But I want you—only you," broke in Kharapet, with a suppressed vehemence, a fierce glitter in his eyes that startled Stasie, her nerves being already a little strained. "I have ever thought of you as mine, and looked to you, and waited for you ; and if you be not my wife neither shall you be the wife of any other. You shall not mock me, I am resolved, without paying dear for your sport ! Once more, Stasie, choose between my love and hate ! "

" I should be very angry with you for talking such nonsense," cried Stasie, " only I see you are disturbed in some unusual way. I do not think you know what you are saying, and I am sorry for it. But if you ever speak in this way again I'll tell my guardian, and never let you inside the doors any more. Why, you must have lost your senses ! " She was angry and frightened both.

Kharapet was silent for a moment or two, the fire died out of his eyes, his face showed a deadly dusky pallor, his hands, which hung down, clenched themselves, while he muttered, in a thick, low tone, " On your head be it ! "

There was a pause. Kharapet turned and went softly towards the door ; then he stopped, and again, facing Stasie, said slowly, " Yes, I have forgotten myself. I have lost my self-control. I ought not to have offended you. You cannot perhaps even imagine the terrible temptation that came over me. Can you forgive? I promise never again to offend. I will go away— away for a long time. You will forgive me, Stasie?"

"I will, I will; only never speak like this again, and do, do go away. I do not like to make you unhappy, but I cannot listen to such wild words any more."

She slipped past him and flew to her own room, where she locked herself in, and indulged in a long, irrepressible fit of sobbing and passionate tears.

Kharapet's looks and manner, as well as his speech, had roused an extraordinary degree of fear and repulsion. How she hoped and prayed he would go away! A sense of being helpless and unprotected oppressed her. Mr. Harding was evidently of little avail; Mrs. Harding, Aunt Clem, powerless; her guardian in some inaccessible region; Mrs. Mathews weak and poor! It was some time before she could compose herself sufficiently to join her aunt, when she found to her relief that Kharapet had gone to dine with Mr. Robinson and Dr. Brooke.

At least he had the good taste not to force himself upon her. How she wished she might never see him again, for in her inmost heart a sudden revelation told her he was a bitter and implacable enemy.

CHAPTER VIII.

Now that the evenings closed in early, Mr. Harding's ardour for his country quarters abated considerably. The walk up from the station of a dark drizzling night was exceedingly disagreeable, and the house, which in long fine days was quite large enough with its supplementary porch and garden, seemed too contracted to breathe in, when shut up at half-past five or six o'clock. This sense of inconvenience made him contradictory and irritable for a day or two before he could confess to having changed his plans.

"This room is either so stuffy that one is smothered, or so cold that one is perished," he said, after changing his seat once or twice, "I think I took cold walking up from the station this evening in the rain."

The dinner had just been cleared away, and the husband and wife were still sitting at table.

" Perhaps you had better take some hot brandy and water instead of wine," said Mrs. Harding.

" Perhaps I had, and, Jane, give me the paper, I had no time to look at it to-day. After all, a life like mine is perfect slavery, toil, toil, toil, for others to spend. What good do I get of my earnings ? "

" You have what most men work for, a comfortable home," returned his wife. " What more can any man, be he ever so rich, get out of his wealth but food, clothes, lodging, and some personal indulgences, besides the consideration of his fellows, which counts for a good deal."

" Ay ! a man whose pockets are well lined is always respected," said Harding complacently, and added, after a pause during which Jane placed the materials requisite for the medicine his wife recommended on the table, " you have a good deal more sense than you used to have, Livy."

" You flatter me," she returned gravely, " you see I have been your pupil now for quite eleven years."

" That's it,—you are right ! " with a tone of

superiority, " and you have been deucedly hard to teach."

" No doubt ; but you have quite succeeded."

Mr. Harding gave an inarticulate grunt of uncertain import, and applied himself to his paper. Mrs. Harding continued to crochet a warm vest for Willie, and silence reigned for some minutes. Then Mr. Harding threw down his paper with disgust.

" I never read such blank, blank nonsense," he exclaimed, " filling whole columns with this bosh about the Education Act. I don't know what we are coming to ! I am pretty sure that if every ploughboy and mechanic is to be taught reading and writing, and the Lord knows what, we'll have the whole edifice about our ears, and the devil to pay into the bargain."

It is scarce necessary to say that Mr. Harding was highly conservative, keenly alive to the necessity of rising himself, and of keeping his inferiors down.

" Is there any Eastern news ? " asked Mrs. Harding, who had long ago given up all idea of arguing with her husband.

" Not much ; I see there are one or two

failures in the tea trade. Things are not what they used to be in China, nor, for that matter, in India either. In my opinion, when matters are a little settled in Japan, *that* will be the place for an enterprising fellow. If Johnnie grows up as I expect he will, I'll establish a house for him out there."

"It will be a good opening, I suppose."

"I believe you,"—another pause, broken suddenly by an exclamation from Mr. Harding. "I say! do you know that Kharapet has been down here for a couple of days?"

"Yes, I saw him at Limeville yesterday."

"And he never came near us! It is most extraordinary. I heard of him from Brooke whom I met coming from Stasie Verner's house. What do you think that Syrian thief is up to?"

"I am sure I haven't the least idea. I imagine he has quite given up all hopes of Stasie?"

"And I am pretty sure he has *not.*"

"Why?"

"Because he is so d—d particular about the investment and management of Stasie's money! He worries my life out; no man would give him-

self so much trouble about what he did not consider his own, or pretty sure to be his own."

"It never will be his, I am convinced," said
Mrs. Harding quietly.

"So am I; but tell me, Livy, how does young
Pearson stand with her?"

"It is hard to say. I am inclined to think
he has not much chance."

"So much the better. It will suit her *and*
me all the more if she does not marry for a
couple of years. By the way, I want to ask
Robinson and your cousin, and Stasie and that
aunt of hers up to dinner on the 15th,—it's my
birthday,—and then we'll go away up to town.
This is a miserable place now winter is creeping
on us."

"Very well," said Mrs. Harding, "I will
begin to prepare."

"And write a line to Dr. Baring; we'll have
Johnnie home for a few days to drink my health."

"I do not think that would be wise," said the
mother gently, "he has hardly had time to settle
since he went to school, and you know from
what the doctor says he has been a little difficult
to manage."

"The doctor is a blank psalm-singing old beggar! he is trying to break the boy's spirit, and *I* want him! So just sit down and write as I tell you."

"I cannot be accessory to what I disapprove," returned Mrs. Harding firmly; "and if you reflect, I think you will see I am right!"

"I shall see nothing of the kind. It is for *me* to judge. Just you sit down without more talk, and write to the doctor."

"No," said Mrs. Harding, "I will not. I have as good a right to decide what is best for my boy as you have, especially at his present age."

Mr. Harding paused a moment thunderstruck, and then, throwing the end of his cigar into the fire, started from his seat and began marching up and down the room in a fury. "I wonder if he will beat me," thought Mrs. Harding, while she kept a cool exterior.

"Do you know what you are about, contradicting me in this way!" he stuttered in a transport of rage. "By—— I believe you have lost your senses! Who pays for the boy? who has a right to decide anything respecting him but me ? By—— I'll have him home, if it were only to show you your place."

"It is my place to insist on what is for his good, and I *will*." Her voice, low and clear, struck Harding with curious effect, as a new force with which he had yet to reckon.

" Have you thought of the consequences—the serious consequences of your —— opposition to my will, your —— obstinacy."

"No, but let us consider them. What can be the result of my maintaining my own opinion as to what is good for my own child ? You cannot put me out of doors for differing from you. You cannot prove me failing in duty or in any way free yourself from the cost of supporting me, to say nothing of losing the cheapest upper servant you could possibly find ; and what about the opinion of your world ? which is worth something. Pooh ! my dear, do not waste your energy getting into a senseless rage ; try to understand your real position. I *have* been hard to teach, as you say, but I have learned my lesson at last. Do sit down—it worries me to see you raging to and fro like a caged bear."

Mr. Harding was so astonished that he did

sit down.   His wife, nearly as much surprised at her own courage, which grew as she spoke, and as she observed the impression she made upon her husband, went on quietly with her work though her heart beat, and her fingers trembled.

" This—this is very extraordinary," exclaimed Mr. Harding at length. " I don't understand you, Livy ! what are you driving at ; what the deuce do you want ? "

" Nothing that is not my due, and that, believe me, I *will* have."

" Who wants to defraud you ! I am sure I am a good husband, and you have never wanted for anything ; and now, this poor boy ! You do not care to see him.   I believe you do not love him because he is like me."

Mrs. Harding laughed a low peculiar laugh, as she thought how gladly she would obliterate all trace of the father from her boy ; but she said, " I should be well pleased to see him resemble you in some respects, not all, and as to loving him, poor fellow ! ask *him* what he thinks !"

" You don't want him to resemble me in all respects, hey ! that is a pretty speech for a wife to make ! Pray, in what respect would you wish him different from me ? "

" In temper and love of self."

" By Jove ! I am a brute, am I ?—a selfish brute ? " Mrs. Harding was silent. " Come, answer me ; am I a selfish brute ?"

" Yes, very often," returned Mrs. Harding emphatically.

" The devil I am ! do you think I care for your opinion."

" I do not know ; but if you convey the same impression to others, it may be inconvenient."

" Well, I must say this is an extraordinary speech from a woman I took without a rag to her back or sixpence in her pocket ! "

" My poverty has nothing to do with my opinions. I do not dispute the imprudence of your choice ; but here I am, and you will find it more to your comfort to treat your wife with decent consideration than to *try* to wipe your feet upon her."

" Oh ! if you are going into the heroics, I have done ! but," rising with an attempt at his usual swagger, " I will have that boy home for the 15th; I'll be d—d if I haven't. I can write to the doctor myself, I suppose ?"

"You can do what you choose, but *I* will take no part in what I object to so strongly."

Mr. Harding hesitated, and then, muttering something about a "devilish obstinate little virago," left the room, slamming the door, beyond which Mrs. Harding heard him shouting to Jane to bring another glass of hot brandy and water to his room.

She put down her work, and, leaning her elbows on the table, buried her face in her hand, a slight shiver passing through her delicate frame. "It is a desperate miserable battle," she thought, "but I must fight it out, and even victory will not release me from degradation, but he shall never trample me under his feet again."

.   .   .   .   .

Kharapet's outbreak made a deep impression on Stasie : not even his departure the following evening relieved her of the strange nervous dread he had evoked. She began to fear she knew not what : to be alone, to be spoken to suddenly, to go out, to stay in, a curious feverish restlessness consumed her strength and painful dreams alternated with intervals of wakefulness through the night. Yet she bore up bravely. She was strong and reasonable, and Brooke, in his daily visits, noticed with deep sympathy and warm admiration the resistance she made against irritability and depression, the sweetness with which she sought to atone for any little outbreak of impatience, the force she exerted to subdue or bear her nervous disturbance. As to himself, a new power of insight of assimilation seemed to be granted him during this terrible and trying time. He managed to propitiate Aunt Clem ; he made himself more acceptable to Mr. Harding than before. He grew all and all to Stasie. From the moment he entered the room, where she sat trying to work, or play some favourite morsel of music, she was aware of a sense of relief. He always suggested some topic that interested her, and drew her out of herself ; and when he bade her good-bye she could hardly restrain herself from crying, " Stay, do not leave me ! " an impulse quite distinct from the shy tenderness which she could not eradicate, and which sprang from the sense of comfort and safety conveyed by his presence.

"What has become of young Pearson?" asked Brooke one afternoon, as he sat talking with the aunt and niece, having vainly attempted to persuade them to come out. "I have not seen him for a long time."

"No; he has quite deserted us," returned Aunt Clem briskly. "I cannot say I deeply regret it. He is very shallow, and not too well bred."

"Well, I liked him very much," cried Stasie. "He is very young, I mean young in nature, but he is bright and pleasant."

"Probably he is away on leave," said Brooke.

"No," replied Miss Stretton. "I saw him at Waterloo Station, and he all but cut me; nothing could be more stiff and awkward than his manner."

Brooke looked towards Stasie and caught her eyes; she coloured quickly, vividly, and with a thrill of delight he took in the situation. Young Pearson had been rejected, and Stasie had honourably kept the secret. Here was a possible obstacle swept from his path; dare he now risk his own fate and hers? He scarcely knew, he felt dizzy for a half second. Stasie's extreme reticence, born of her fear of displaying feelings which were not to be reciprocated, held him back, and she too was misled by her strong conviction—first, that Brooke was attached to his cousin; secondly, that his interest in herself was professional.

Meanwhile Miss Stretton was talking on steadily. "I cannot say I think Stasie much improved," she was saying when Brooke next listened to her. "She is decidedly thinner and more languid. I am rather anxious for next Wednesday; we are going to see Sir Harcourt, and if he suggests nothing new, I should certainly recommend homœopathy."

"Yes, it would do as well as anything else," replied Brooke, out of his thoughts, and not heeding his words.

"Do you then despair of me?" cried Stasie quickly, her large eyes very wide open, and dewy with something like tears.

"Despair? no," drawing near her and leaning on the back of her chair. "I wish I could persuade you to consult *me*. I have the secret of

the true remedy, but you do not believe in
me!"

"Believe or not, I will ask your help if I am
not better soon."

"The fact is, Stasie so often forgot her medicine at first, and, I am ashamed to say, so did I
(you see I have *so* much to attend to, so many
cares on my mind, Dr. Brooke), that Mr. Kharapet, with his usual sound judgment, advised me
to entrust——"

Here she was interrupted by the entrance of
Bhoodhoo, who held a small salver on which
stood a wine glass containing about a spoonful
of greenish white fluid, and a caraffe of water.

"Ah, just so! here he is, as punctual as the
sun," concluded Miss Stretton, smiling on him.
The Hindoo approached Stasie with a slight
bow; filling up the glass with water he presented
it to her, and stood calmly watching while she
drank it off and returned the glass. He then
set down the tray on a table by the door, made
up the fire, put the chairs in order—all softly,
noiselessly—took up his tray again and departed.

Brooke stood straight up, with a sudden fresh
fear thrilling through his veins.

" Did Kharapet advise you to confide the administration of Miss Verner's medicine to that —— man ? " he asked.

" Yes ; why should he not ? " said Stasie, struck by his tone.

" I don't know, only it seems to me more natural that your own maid should do this service."

" Oh ! no one is to be depended on like Bhood-hoo," cried Miss Stretton. " He is so thought-ful, so attentive ! "

Brooke was struck dumb at the sight of such a means of destruction placed in the hands of Stasie's enemies. Had he been alone with her he would then and there have risked all, and asked her to be his wife. He felt he could not endure this state of things much longer, and that for the moment he must get away and speak to some one, even in a half confidence.

He walked to the window and back. Stasie felt he was deeply disturbed; she could not understand why. Why should he be put out because Bhoodhoo brought her her medicine ?

" I must leave you ; I have not seen Mrs. Harding since the day before yesterday. Miss

Verner, if I may come to-morrow I will read you some bits from my rough notes of an expedition I made into Cashmere; they may amuse you."

"Oh yes, do come," cried Stasie, more warmly than she was aware.

Brooke left the house and walked rapidly towards Mrs. Harding's abode in a maddening state of alarm and indecision. The net was closing round Stasie, the danger growing more imminent. He could not banish from his eyes the picture of her fair, frank face, her kindly smile of thanks, as she put out her hand to take perhaps her death from the dark traitor she had loaded with kindness. How willingly and easily Brooke would have crushed his life out, if he did not know that any overt act of his would have cut off Stasie's only chance of escape.

He must not delay any longer. He must avow his love for her, and strive to gain her consent to an immediate marriage. Even this, if successful, was full of danger and difficulty. If Kharapet knew of such a project being on foot, he could soon snap the delicate cords that bound his victim to life! Then even punishment would be scare possible, and if it were, what consolation could that afford? what could earth give to supply the loss of a creature that had grown so inexpressibly dear to him, who had revealed to him possibilities of joy and sorrow of which he had never previously dreamed.

His burning anxiety for her safety and welfare had given something of a father's tenderness and consideration to his love for her, yet there were moments when danger seemed less pressing, or Stasie herself seemed more than usually confiding, when a sudden sense of her beauty and unconscious grace thrilled him with passionate intoxicating delight, and made him fearful of his own eagerness; for affection such as his is always self-distrustful. And she was so young, so inexperienced; how could he tell that extended knowledge of society might not show her many whom she would prefer to himself?

That she began to trust and lean upon him he perceived, and had he time, he might possibly win her love. She was proud and delicate; suppose a sudden declaration were to frighten away the first soft gathering mists of tenderness, hereafter to descend upon him in a golden shower of bounteous love! If he failed, he must warn her, remove her at any risk. "The way to safety, the only secure way, is to me such a heaven of hope that my calmer sense reels. I must think for her alone."

By this time he had passed Sefton House considerably, walking with long swift strides, too feverish and disturbed to heed where he was going, when he found himself suddenly confronted by the very person he sought.

"Why, Jim, are you walking for a wager?"

"No, I was lost in thought, and I was coming to see you."

"Then you have considerably overshot the mark," said Mrs. Harding, smiling; "we are quite half a mile from home."

"I am afraid I took no heed of time or space either," replied Brooke, turning with her; "must you go straight back, or can you come round by the copse and the rector's fields? I want a very private consultation with you."

"And I with you. No, I need not return just yet. I have been down to Frome's house (the man who manages our small farming operations) with a message from Mr. Harding, and he was out; let us go round by the path and try to find him again. Now, begin your tale, Jim."

" I prefer hearing yours first."

" Well, there are one or two matters I wish to speak to you about. First, what is most important and interesting to you ! I am growing very uneasy about Stasie Verner."

" Ha !" cried Brooke, with deeply stirred attention.

" She is getting into such a nervous state—so unlike herself—that I do not know what to make of her. She is conscious that her fears and fancies are unreal, and yet she cannot master them."

" How ?" ejaculated Brooke.

" I will tell you, though it is a breach of confidence. Yesterday she paid me a long visit, and we were alone, which seldom happens. Gradually she came to talk of Hormuz Kharapet, and I was quite distressed at the curious unreasoning terror of him she, at first, half-unconsciously displayed ; then she opened her heart, and I gathered that he had made a violent scene some days ago—a scene that has produced an extraordinary impression on her, quite inadequate to the cause. She seems to dread and detest him. I really think she ought to go away somewhere for a while ; but if she goes with Miss Stretton, of course that entails constant visits from Kharapet."

" Go on ! " exclaimed Brooke. Mrs. Harding glanced at him and continued : " I think Stasie will have a bitter enemy in Kharapet when he realises that she will never marry him. Mr. Harding said the other evening that he must look on Stasie's money as his own : he is so careful about investing and managing it."

" Is he ? the infernal villain," ejaculated Brooke, with a force that startled his hearer.

" I do not know that you can help us in any way, Jim—especially as Stasie is averse to consult you professionally, though she is certainly uneasy about herself ; but it is a comfort to talk to you."

" No ; I know but too well how little use I can be," said Brooke, "unless—indeed"——he paused.

" My dear Jim, are you not too distrustful of yourself ? "

" Do you venture to encourage me, Livy ? Your opinion has great weight with me. Do you think I have any chance ? "

" In truth I cannot tell ; but were you accepted, you would be a tower of strength——"

" And were I rejected, all would be lost."

" Yes, for you ; but I am so anxious that Stasie should like—love you—that perhaps my wishes stimulate my hopes. After my own children, you and Stasie are the only creatures I care for in the world."

" Thank you, my dear cousin ; believe me, it is more than the mere dread of rejection on my own account that holds me back ; one day"—but interrupting himself—" I will risk it, Livy, on the first opportunity—dread of one suitor may drive poor Miss Verner into the arms of another. Should she accept me, our marriage must be immediate."

" I do not see that ! " exclaimed Mrs. Harding ; "your position as an accepted suitor would entitle you to exercise influence, and even authority."

"And how soon would Kharapet and Wyatt and your husband admit my claim to either ? " asked Brooke grimly.

Mrs. Harding's eyes met his, and she seemed to take in some unspoken communication, at which her colour rose faintly, and, after a pause, she said low, but very distinctly :

" Should you ever consider any extra prompt measures necessary—which I do not think will be the case—do not tell me. However heartily I may sympathise with you both, it would not do for me to connive at any—let us say unconventional—proceedings in my own relative. I must *ménager* my husband, you know, Jim ; and indeed—indeed—once accepted, there would be no need for unbecoming haste.'

"No need for haste!" repeated Brooke absently. "We shall see ; at any rate, Livy, I shall always count on your friendship—your good-will, may I not?"

"You may indeed," softly. There was a long pause, during which Mrs. Harding stole a glance at her companion's face. She was struck by the look of resolution, sombre and set, which had come into it. His deep, dark eyes were wide opened, with a far-off look, as if he were reviewing his scattered but available forces. At length his companion broke the silence : "You think me a dreadful coward, no doubt, Jim."

"Who—me?" cried Brooke, coming back from his mental excursions. "No! I wonder your brain and nerves are not in a state of liquifaction, considering the burning fiery furnace through which you have passed."

"I have not had a very happy life, but it is going to be better—I am going to make it better," in a quietly firm tone.

"I am delighted to hear it; and I believe there is much in your own power."

"Yes, and the power is coming, as I have lived through fear and hope, and that terrible longing for sympathy that does not exist. I have won another battle since I last had a quiet talk with you, Jim," and she described the struggle she had had with her husband respecting a supernumerary holiday for Johnnie.

Brooke listened with sincere interest. "I am glad you won, Livy," he said; "but were you right to contradict him about the boy? His best point is his affection—such as it is—for the children. It was better Johnnie should stay at school, but——"

"It was," interrupted Mrs. Harding, "and still more necessary for me to insist upon his remaining there. My dear Jim, in a contest such as I have entered upon, I must *never* yield. I will be very careful, if I can, not to take the *wrong* side in any dispute; but once I have adopted a side, I must maintain it at all costs."

"I am very glad you have taken my advice, Livy."

"Yes, your words strengthened me, but the idea was dawning on me; and the irresistible appeal of the children, to whom I felt my emancipation was all-important, gave me courage. The first steps of an insurrection are always the most difficult, I suppose. The first time I disputed Mr. Harding's dictum was a supreme effort, but the second was infinitely easier. I shall conquer, Jim, in the end; for, having nothing to lose, I can dare all things. My supremacy will be a boon to my husband as well as to my children, if I win it. I look back at my past cowardice with shame and contrition—but better late than never."

"No doubt," replied Brooke; "you have inserted the thin edge of the wedge; all you have to do now is to strike home."

"I ought to tell you," concluded Mrs. Harding, with a smile, "that the night before last Mr. Harding informed me, with an air of authority, he had made up his mind not to have Johnnie home for the 15th, and that I was *not* to write to Dr. Baring. I answered meekly, "Very well," and so the matter ended. I wonder what our next battle will be about?"

" No matter; nail your colours to the mast; I see you are right. In such a contest you must neither give nor take quarter."

" And God defend the right!" concluded Mrs. Harding, with a smile, half sad and slightly mocking.

CHAPTER IX.

MR. HARDING'S change of plans threw a gloom
over the little circle at Sefton Park. Mrs.
Harding was tacitly looked upon as its head and
centre ; but the prospect of her departure woke
up in each member a sudden sense of her value
and importance.

To Stasie the prospect of her removal from
the immediate neighbourhood was peculiarly
depressing. Though attached to her aunt, she
could never find the companionship and suffi-
ciency she needed in her society, while Mrs.
Harding amply supplied both.

The knowledge that within a few hundred
yards was household warmth, ready kindly greeting, the cheery rippling of children's voices and
laughter, a friendly sympathetic listener whose
simple straight-forward common-sense was always
at the service of those that sought counsel or

advice, was wonderfully comforting and strengthening ; and to think of that homely familiar abode closed, its pleasant windows shuttered, its comfortable chimneys smokeless, its hearth-stones cold, was intolerably oppressive.

Miss Stretton, observing the effect this approaching separation produced upon her niece, and beginning to think Sefton Park might probably be a dreary residence in winter, suddenly suggested that they might as well terminate their tenancy of Limeville in the ensuing month of November, and move to town into a furnished house, "for," concluded the thoughtful spinster, "after being accustomed to your own nice servants, my love, you would not like to put up with what you would find in a lodging. I will just write and ask Mr. Kharapet to come down and talk it over ; it is curious that neither he nor Mr. Pearson have been near us for a week past."

Stasie said she would like to go to town very much, and then reminded her aunt that more than a fortnight had elapsed since her first visit to Sir Harcourt Filmer, and that it would be well to pay him another, as she did not think herself much the better for his remedies.

To this proposition Aunt Clem eagerly agreed, and the following day was fixed upon.

To Brooke this move brought little or no hope. His interview with Filmer proved how little there was to expect either from his knowledge or his imagination ; yet he resolved to see him once more, and ascertain from his own lips his opinion of the young patient.

In the interim he had seen Stasie nearly every day, and though he had watched her narrowly, he perceived nothing to increase his alarm. She was paler, stiller, more apt to start and tremble on slight occasions. Her eyes, too, had the strained and slightly staring look that always distressed him.

For the last few days she had by his advice left off taking Sir Harcourt's prescription. This was a little relief ; but Brooke too was cast down by the prospect of Mrs. Harding's departure. He felt so sure of a faithful intelligent ally, so far as he could trust her, that her loss appeared irreparable. How could he get on when she was too far for daily, hourly communication ? However, a conviction—a calming and strengthening conviction—was growing upon

him that this state of things could not last long,
that he must soon find an opportunity to put an
end to it.

However, he availed himself once more of his
friendly relations with Filmer to call on the day
following Stasie's visit, when he held a brief conversation with his old master.

"I cannot say I find her improved," admitted
Sir Harcourt. "I begin to suspect that the case
is a little more complicated than I imagined.
The heart certainly seems weak, and there is
considerable depression ; but I still think the
same prescription, a little varied, and persevered
in, may give relief. I have told her to go on
with it for another fortnight, and then to return
to me."

"If she still survives," put in Brooke quietly.

"My good fellow, are you still harping on
that poisoning theory of yours ? Believe me, it
is a hallucination. I have thought it over as I
would not have done had it been propounded by
any other man than yourself, and I feel quite sure
it will not hold water. Let your young friend
follow my directions, and have a little change
of air ; you'll see she will come round."

"I will take care she does," said Brooke, with grim resolution.

"Pray do, if you can suggest a better course of treatment."

When Brooke left his former master he felt none of the agitated despair that racked him after their first interview. He was calm, with the strength of a clear and fixed decision. He would, on the first opportunity, ask Stasie to be his wife; if she refused, then he would tell her, and her only, of his fears for her life. Even if she objected to him as a husband, he thought there was sufficient sympathy and understanding between them to make her trust him as a friend, as a man who would not speak unadvisedly or yield belief too readily. She too was brave and strong; and if she would but confide in him he might save her—save her to be happy with some luckier fellow than himself. Brooke indulged in no mental heroics over this magnanimous idea. His ardent desire to save a young precious life, possessed of all possibilities for good and happiness, swallowed up every thought of self; only, *if* she would accept the safety which the position of his wife would give her! Why, the idea made

him dizzy with delight—so dizzy that he determined to keep it out of his head as much as
possible. But should Stasie reject both his suit
and his suspicions, how would it be? It was a
tremendous risk.

Even if she accepted him, how should he persuade her to take so daring, so desperate a step
as to elope! One of her greatest charms was a
peculiar, proud, frank modesty that would certainly hold her back from such a step, unless, indeed, frightened into it; and he especially wished
to avoid startling her by any revelation of the
danger which surrounded her in her own quiet
home. However terrible the alternative, he must
risk an avowal, and be guided by what it brought
forth.

The dread with which Kharapet seemed to
have inspired Stasie, according to Mrs. Harding's
account, might help him, and he would for the
present hope the best.

The second visit to Sir Harcourt Filmer did
not appear to have produced so depressing an
effect as the first, though Stasie was very pale
and quiet that evening, when Brooke went in to
pay them a visit, as Mr. Robinson had gone out

to dine with the father of the young lady whose attractions had raised such a struggle in his priestly mind.

But she told him with some animation that Kharapet was coming down to arrange with Miss Stretton for a move to town.

"I am quite glad about it," added Stasie, who was sitting in a low basket-chair near the fire, playing idly with Pearl's ear. (She had grown strangely indolent of late.) "Now that the Hardings are going, I feel as if I could not stay here. It seems dreadfully whimsical, for I was quite fond of this place at first, but now I feel anxious to leave it. It would kill me to stay."

"You will be much better away," remarked Brooke, who was standing on the hearth-rug, and gazing at her downcast eyes, and the long lashes which rested on her cheek; and remember, Miss Verner, I claim your promise to accept my advice if Filmer fails."

"I confess I have not much faith in him," said Stasie, raising her eyes to his, and colouring quickly, as she met them in a way quite unusual to her, which showed Brooke that his said more than he imagined. "At present I feel tolerably well; but if I am ill again I *will* ask your advice, Dr. Brooke, for you only seem to see that I am or have been really ill. As for Sir Harcourt Filmer——"

"My dearest Stasie!" cried Aunt Clem, interrupting her with some emotion, "do not say that! I am sure Dr. Brooke himself has seen the deep, deep anxiety that I have felt on your account. I am now convinced that this dreadful, damp, desolate place is killing you! So I have begged Mr. Kharapet to come down and consult with me. It *is* so difficult to catch Mr. Harding, or get him to attend to anything; and now that he is full of his own move, he is worse than ever. But I am sure Mr. Kharapet will arrange everything for the best. I have the greatest confidence in him."

A slight smile passed over Stasie's lips; and after a moment's silence she exclaimed, "Don't you think, auntie, you are so much better now, we might go to France or Italy?"

"I am sure, my dear Stasie, nothing would give me greater pleasure; but I must see Dr. Grimond, and ascertain if I dare undertake a journey. It would never do for you to be

troubled dragging an invalid all over the continent of Europe."

" You must be all right yourself, Miss Verner,
before you attempt the grand tour," said Brooke,
who could not shake off the impression which
Stasie's quick conscious blush had made upon
him. He longed for an enchanter's wand to
transport Miss Stretton away anywhere, that he
might be alone with Stasie, to clasp her hands
and read the truth of her heart through her sweet
honest eyes, to plead with her, to warn her !
He stood there absorbed, deaf to a continuous
stream of babble which Miss Stretton poured
forth, seeking in vain for another glance from
eyes that generally said so much. But in vain.
Stasie soon after rose and changed her seat, and
Brooke, finding the restraint on the expression of
his feelings intolerable, bade them good-night.

" I really do think he is very clever," said
Aunt Clem, looking after him as the door closed;
" and, joking apart, he might suggest something
that would do you good. He is most polite and
considerate to me too. I wonder how he and
Mrs. Harding are getting on ? or if Mr. H.
is a little jealous ! He does not go nearly so

often to Sefton House as he used, but that may
be a blind!"

"I wish you would not talk in that way, Aunt
Clem! it is too vulgar. Dr. Brooke may be
fond of Mrs. Harding, but——"

"Vulgar!" interrupted Miss Stretton, somewhat indignantly. "Well, Stasie, that is the last
accusation I should ever have expected from *you*,
nor am I aware that I used any unladylike expression. Indeed, my dear child, I do not admit
that you are a competent judge; for though you
have an excellent disposition and all that, you
are decidedly deficient in that sense of propriety,
that elegant self-possession, which I have en-
deavoured to inculcate on you." Miss Stretton
paused with dignity.

"I know I am not genteel!" cried Stasie,
and I beg your pardon if I spoke rudely.
I did not mean you were vulgar in words or
manner, that you never are, only——" she
stopped.

"Only in thought! I am much obliged to
you!" cried Miss Stretton. "However, vulgar
or not, they understand each other. It is only
three or four days ago since I watched them out

of the staircase-window coming down the avenue, so utterly absorbed in each other that Thorn's boy—the butcher at Welwood—had to drive quite to one side, on the grass, to avoid running over them, they never seemed to hear or see the horse or cart."

Stasie made no reply, and Miss Stretton, mollified by the sound of her own voice, continued. "As to going abroad, I really should like it well enough, and it's a curious thing, Stasie, that when trying the cards for *you*, dear (you see I think of you, though I *am* a vulgar person), it was as plain as the nose on your face that you are to go across the sea to escape a dark man! but who it is I cannot think. Mr. Pearson is fair, and so is Mr. Robinson, and it *could* not be Dr. Brooke; he does not seem to care enough about any one except Mrs. Harding to do mischief, though he is very gentlemanlike and well bred.

"Might it not be Mr. Kharapet," suggested Stasie, with a faint mischievous smile.

"Mr. Kharapet! our best friend!" cried Aunt Clem. "Ah! Stasie, I am afraid those Pearson people have turned your head, for I observe your manner has been quite different to that kind good man since you came back from Southsea; and he is worth a dozen, nay dozens of that conceited young Pearson.

.   .   .   .   .

The following day was a protracted penance to Brooke. He found Kharapet installed at Limeville, and the whole house redolent of curry. Aunt Clem, in her best cap and sweetest smiles, was far too much occupied with the favoured guest to bestow much attention on Brooke, and Stasie was not visible; so he wandered about the park and comforted himself by a long talk with Mrs. Harding.

Mr. Robinson, who had presented a very cheerful aspect since his dinner at Mr. Morison's, was disposed to be communicative as the friends sat together in the evening.

"I am sorry they did not ask you, Brooke," said the young clergyman. "They are really a very nice family, Mrs. Morison is so kind and motherly, and the young ladies are very accomplished. They are rich too. The father has not had the same educational advantages as his children, but he is a liberal-minded man.

He takes a great interest in the church. I mean this church here, and is planning some means with my Uncle Williams (he is my uncle by marriage) to raise funds for a stone edifice. I am to meet them at Mr. Williams's office to-morrow to talk the matter over. Three more houses have been let lately—one of these large houses and two villas—so the congregation will be considerably increased." The Rev. St. John paused, evidently not for want of words or subject.

"And the young lady you talked to me about that day at Richmond is one of his daughters?" asked Brooke taking his cigar from his mouth and laying down his book, as he saw his host was disposed to be confidential. "What is this Morison?"

"Oh! he has a huge ready-made clothes warehouse in the borough."

"What! like Moses?"

"No, no; ladies' clothes, bonnets, flowers, all sorts of things. He is evidently inclined to be very liberal about the church; and, do you know, Brooke, I have thought very seriously and conscientiously respecting the question of marriage for a priest. After all, I begin to think that family life is the holiest of all! especially when one can find a helpmeet so devout, so eager to assist in all good works, so sweetly cheerful, so kind-hearted as Marion Morison."

"If she is all that, you ought not to let her slip through your fingers," said Brooke, smiling, as he looked at the beaming face of his former schoolfellow.

"I really think it would be weak and unwise. I have hitherto been deterred by a consciousness of my own narrow circumstances and insignificance — at least personal insignificance — of course the dignity of my calling is apart—nothing can touch *that*. But, do you know, Brooke,—I may be mistaken,—it struck me last night, that somehow Mr. Morison would not object to me as a son-in-law, and that his interest in the church somehow is growing a personal matter."

"Very likely. The biggest haberdasher in London might be glad to get a clergyman of the Church of England, and a right good fellow to boot, for a son-in-law. Go in and win, my dear boy!"

"I must not be too sure, you know, Brooke. I shall know more to-morrow. Indeed, I feel a little nervous about the meeting."

"Faint heart never won fair lady! I can't go with you to this council of three, Robby, but I will go into town with you. I hate meeting that fellow Kharapet, and I suppose he will be here all to-morrow."

"I think you are unreasonably prejudiced, Brooke."

"Reasonably or unreasonably. I'd like to wring his neck," said Brooke with vindictive energy, that startled and shocked his friend, who, after a pause, resumed their conversation, which soon branched off to topics unconnected with this story.

Brooke found occupation enough in visiting his club, reading and answering some letters which he found there, and executing one or two commissions contained in one of them, to employ him till evening had closed in; and he met Robinson at the station in time to return with him to Sefton Park by the last train but one.

Robinson was still radiant. He explained at great length, and not too clearly, a complicated scheme by which Mr. Williams proposed to raise money sufficient to build the church, and he (Robinson) was charged with the inspection and selection of plans, etc.

Brooke was not profoundly attentive. His thoughts were occupied with the question, Was he right to absent himself for so many hours at a stretch? He was filled with a fear that some untoward circumstance might arise in which, were he on the spot, he might be of use to Stasie or Mrs. Harding. He was curiously uneasy. He was filled with burning anxiety to know if Kharapet had left or would prolong his visit.

"Did you see anything of Kharapet to-day?" asked Brooke, taking advantage of a pause in Robinson's ready flowing talk.

"No; I fancy he is staying down here. Mrs. Harris tells me Miss Stretton's native servant came over to ask for a few bay leaves to flavour something, and that looks like more than the two ladies themselves to dinner."

"Ha! very likely. What o'clock is it, Robby?"

"Half-past eight."

"Not too late to have a word with Harding

before I turn in ;" so saying Brooke rose, took his hat and went forth. It was a still dark night, full of the autumnal scent of some pine-trees, of which a clump stood a little higher up the road, of the faint odour of freshly-turned earth from a newly ploughed field. No lamps as yet illuminated the chief approach to Sefton House, but Brooke knew the way well, and crossed to the opposite side of the way, as the path there was more worn and smoother. As he approached Limeville he observed lights in two of the upper rooms.

"I wonder if Kharapet has bored Stasie to death, and she has beat an early retreat," thought Brooke, as his imagination pictured the soft subtle Syrian, whose conversational powers, beyond certain subjects, were limited, indulging himself in furtive glances either of admiration or hate—or both in one—or playing draughts with Miss Stretton, a game in which he rather excelled. These thoughts brought him within a few steps of the gate, when it opened, and a murmur of voices caught his ear; two men were speaking, not English. He paused and involuntarily drew close to the paling, for in spite of

the dusky night he recognised Kharapet and
Bhoodhoo.

They spoke low but earnestly, Bhoodhoo ges-
ticulating with what seemed to Brooke's experience an apologetic air. They were speaking
Hindoostance, but Brooke could only catch an
indistinct murmur. There was a sound of re-
buke in Kharapet's accent. After a few paces
Bhoodhoo paused, and Kharapet went on a step,
then half turning, said in a louder tone and
emphatically almost like a threat, "*Khabar-dār.*"
Bhoodhoo bowed low, stepped back, stopped an
instant, and then re-entered the grounds of Limeville, evidently without perceiving the presence
of a third person.

Brooke paused till he heard the gate shut and
locked, he then walked on quickly till within a
safe distance of Kharapet, whom he watched
until he had seen him enter the garden of Sefton
House. He gave up his own intention of paying
Mr. and Mrs. Harding a visit, and, retracing his
steps, strolled as far as the railway station in
deep thought.

"*Khabar-dār.*" He knew the word; it conveyed a warning, "be careful," in the sense of

" not too fast." The tone in which it was uttered gave deeper significance to the syllables.

It might mean anything. That Bhoodhoo should be careful in his service, conscientious. in conduct, or careful in carrying out Kharapet's plans. Was he going too fast with his devilish designs ?

The word haunted Brooke. The terrible anxiety, which his own decision as to his future conduct had allayed for a moment, especially as he considered Kharapet's presence as a kind of guarantee against any immediate catastrophe, woke up with redoubled force. He burned to go straight to Limeville and comfort himself with one look at Stasie before he slept, but that was impossible, it was now considerably past nine.

He walked to and fro for a while, and then returned to the house. Robinson was deep in the composition of his weekly discourse, and after a vain attempt to read, Brooke retired to rest, or rather to unrest.

His first waking thought was of the ill-omened word he had overheard the night before; but thank God it was daylight, and the day was before him. He had not been to Limeville for forty-eight hours, and now he was entitled to pay a visit. He would go as early as politeness permitted. His spirits rose as he dressed and breakfasted, and his sense of relief was completed by seeing Kharapet walking down the road with unusual speed, probably to catch the nine o'clock train, as he was followed by Bhoodhoo, who carried a large travelling-bag.

Brooke wrote a couple of letters, he smoked a cigar, he discussed an article in the *Times* with his friend, he strove to delay and occupy himself in various ways, and yet it was only eleven o'clock when he rang the front door bell at Limeville. The door—now ordinarily closed against the chill autumnal air—was opened by Mary, the neat bright-looking housemaid, whose aspect struck Brooke as unusually grave and serious. "Are the ladies visible?" he asked.

"Yes, sir; leastways Miss Stretton. Miss Verner's not out of her room, sir. She was taken very ill last night."

"Ill, how?" exclaimed Brooke, whose heart stood still for an instant of agony. Had he delayed too long in cowardly dread of losing her? was this the beginning of the end?

"She was taken faint, sir, like she was before, only a good bit worse, and she was awful frightened herself of things coming a-near her, she said."

"Let Miss Stretton know I am here," said Brooke, walking into the well-known drawing-room. "Ask her if she will be so good as to see me."

He felt beside himself for an instant. It took all his power of self-mastery, all his consciousness that on his own courage and coolness everything depended, to control the emotion which shook him.

Miss Stretton did not keep him long waiting. She entered looking wan and worn, as if with watching, her eyes red rimmed and dull.

"Oh! Dr. Brooke, we have had such a fright. I was on the point of sending for you, only they said you were away in London."

"How is she now?" asked Brooke abruptly, and looking at her as if he were ready to devour her words.

"Better, thank God! She has slept quite quietly since between three and four this morning; now she has had some tea and toast, and is reading in bed. I have insisted on her staying there to-day."

" Tell me how she was affected," asked Brooke, drawing a chair near the sofa on which Miss Stretton had sunk.

"We had had quite a happy day. Mr. Kharapet quite went in with my idea of moving to town, and we agreed to go in next week and meet him to look for a house. Stasie was in very good spirits, and talked a little of going on the Continent ; she ate her dinner, and in short was quite herself, when about seven o'clock, when we were having tea, she grew quite silent and still. I didn't mind her, for Mr. Kharapet was giving us a most interesting description of a school for converted Jews at Baghdad, when all of a sudden Stasie stood up and tried to walk towards me, staggering in the strangest way ; then she sat down and said there was a wild black cat in the room that frightened her, and a snake, and caught at the sofa cushions, her hands twitching and her eyes staring awfully. Mr. Kharapet was quite frightened. We tried to give her some brandy, but she could not take it ; then she went into a dead faint and lay insensible, I do not know how long; at last she came to, and we got her to bed. I do not think I ever was so terrified. Of course we sent off for Dr. Hunter, but he had been called. For some time my poor dear Stasie was very uneasy, so terribly giddy she would not let go my hand, at last she fell asleep, and she seems much better than I could have hoped this morning."

"A very extraordinary seizure," said Brooke as she paused; he felt himself grow pale as she described the symptoms which confirmed his worst fears. "What had she eaten?"

"Nothing but roast fowl and a simple pudding; there was curry; she did not take any, which was unusual—and she has taken her medicine quite regularly."

"Will you allow me to see the prescription?" asked Brooke, determined to put an end to *this* danger at any rate.

"Certainly," replied Miss Stretton, who proceeded to unlock the drawer of a writing-table and take out an envelope, which she handed to him; he opened it and read the contents gravely.

"This must be discontinued at present," he

said with authority. " I would not let Miss Verner touch it till she has seen Filmer again."

" Very well," said Miss Stretton submissively.

" Give her something very simple, such as your English cook can prepare, when she needs nourishment." Brooke stopped, overwhelmed with the sense of his own impotence to guard or watch over her. " I wish I could see her; I fancy I might prescribe something myself. I have seen attacks like this "——again he stopped abruptly, just saving himself from adding the words " in India," which, if repeated to Kharapet, might awaken him to the fact that he (Brooke) was on the watch.

" I will go and tell Stasie; she may get up in the afternoon."

Brooke paced the room. This attack explained Kharapet's warning of the night before, " *Khabar-dār!* " Bhoodhoo had been going too fast; the instigator of the crime did not wish the end just yet! When should he see her? when should he have the opportunity of pleading with her, for her life and his own?

" Stasie desires her kind regards; she feels so tired she does not think she will come downstairs to-day; Mrs. Harding is with her just now—she will be glad to see you to-morrow. Do you know, Dr. Brooke, I do not imagine she has an idea how ill she has been; she is talking quite comfortably about moving into town."

"Better she should not think of her own condition," said Brooke. "Keep her as quiet as you can." He took up his hat. "I shall call to inquire in the course of the day, and shall hope to see Miss Verner to-morrow."

It was a relief to be out of the house, to stride across the fields in the open, and then what a crowd of ideas thronged his brain. At all hazards Stasie must be removed, and he began busily to construct the details of a plan by which her flight might be kept secret for a week or two. This was all important, in order that by no legal quibble, no chicanery or twisting of the law as it affects minors, should Stasie be for an hour alone in the presence or power of Kharapet. Sometimes a glimpse of the possible heaven awaiting him beyond the dangers of the present struck him with a lightning flash of almost painful delight.

At last he found himself miles from Limeville,

and, retracing his steps, sought some support in a talk with his cousin. She was deeply concerned about Stasie, but less alarmed than Miss Stretton, not having been present when the attack came on. She was very anxious to know Brooke's opinion, but he committed himself to nothing, waiting to see what to-morrow would bring forth. He called more than once at Limeville, where he was made very welcome by poor Miss Stretton, who was thankful to have a sympathetic listener. Her report of the invalid was better each time. So the weary day wore through.

CHAPTER X.

WHETHER from fatigue or mental exhaustion, Brooke slept better than he had done for weeks that night, and consequently woke calmer, stronger, and less despairing.

While waiting impatiently till it was time to see Stasie, sitting, as was his wont, in a large window which looked upon the main road, he saw, to his surprise, Miss Stretton walking in the direction of the station, with her "rain-cloak" over her arm. He caught up his hat and followed her.

"Ah! Dr. Brooke!" she exclaimed, as he overtook her, "I have a very good report to give you. Stasie is quite like herself this morning. She is up and dressed. She slept well, and has eaten a new-laid egg for her breakfast."

"I am rejoiced to hear it! Are you going to town?"

"Yes. I had quite a consultation with Mrs.

Harding last night. (They have been most kind!) And as dear Stasie is so anxious to leave this, I am going to look at a house and furnished apartments which Mr. Harding saw advertised in the *Times.* I feel quite nervous myself about staying on here. I am sure Stasie will be better and more cheerful in town, so I thought it better to go at once. Mrs. Harding has promised to stay with Stasie."

" Is it too early to call on Miss Verner ? "

"Oh, no! You will rouse her and amuse her. She always enjoys a talk with you."

" I will first see you into the train."

Miss Stretton was flattered, and they talked very amicably together. The timid spinster informed Brooke that she expected Mr. Kharapet to meet and assist her in her choice of a residence. "For, I must confess, Dr. Brooke, I shrink from responsibility."

Having seen Miss Stretton off, Brooke walked at what he intended to be a slow pace towards Limeville, but he soon found himself involuntarily hastening his steps. If Mrs. Harding was already with Stasie, surely she would give him a chance of speaking alone with her ?

But he was at her gate, and this time was admitted by Bhoodhoo, who informed him, with a gentle kindly smile, " that missee Sahib was much better, and so every one was better." Brooke did not trust himself to reply.

Stasie was half-sitting, half-reclining, in her favourite corner of a large old-fashioned sofa, her work-basket beside her, and a book in her hand, She wore a warm winter dress of dark gray; a cravatte of soft old lace round her throat; her hair rather loosely drawn back, showing the graceful curved line of its growth round the temples. She was very pale, and her eyes looked heavy; but she smiled brightly as she held out her hand to him.

" I hope I have not come too early, Miss Verner? but I have been desperately anxious to see you."

His eyes seconded his words; they dwelt on hers eagerly, intensely, compelling them, as it were, to meet his gaze.

" You are very good," she said languidly. " I am really quite well, that is, as well as I have been at any time since I was at Southsea;" she sighed.

"That is not saying much! But are you quite free from giddiness and the unpleasant sensations in your head?"

"Yes, quite. I do not think I was so ill as they fancied, but I feel dull and weak." There was a pause; Brooke drew a chair opposite her, and, looking round, said—"I expected to find Mrs. Harding here."

"I have just had this note from her;" and Stasie, who seemed averse to speak more than she could help, handed it to him, and he read— "DEAREST STASIE—I am very vexed that Mr. Harding wants me to go into town with him to see to some alterations at York Gate. I hope to return early, and will come to you. In the meantime send for Mademoiselle, if you do not like to be alone."

"She must have gone by the nine train," said Brooke, returning the note, "for I have just seen your aunt off, and Mrs. Harding was not there."

"Yes, I fancy this note was forgotten till just now; I have only had it a few minutes."

There was a pause, interrupted by the entrance of Bhoodhoo carrying Pearl, who had just been washed, and was looking miserable. Brooke, by an instinctive movement took the dog, before Bhoodhoo was near the sofa, and held the little creature, who looked up at him trembling from among its long hair.

" Will the missee Sahib have some nice soup presently ? " Brooke listened anxiously for the reply.

" No, thank you, Bhoodhoo ; I shall not want anything till dinner time. I shall not dine till two, for Mrs. Harding or Mademoiselle will dine with me."

Bhoodhoo salaamed and retired.

" This little animal is not half dry," said Brooke, considerably relieved by Stasie's words. " I will put him before the fire. There, Pearl, good dog ! lie still."

Pearl found the warmth very agreeable, and soon settled himself to sleep without further discipline.

Then there was another pause, most oppressive to Brooke, whose heart was too full for words.

At length Stasie, leaning her head languidly against the cushion beside her, said quietly, naturally—"People cannot make wills before they are twenty-one, can they?"

"No! Why do you ask? you do not want to make yours?"

"Yes, I do," looking at him with a pleasant smile. "I should like Mrs. Matthews and Ella to have some of my money if I die."

"But you must not, *shall* not die," cried Brooke with sudden passion, starting up and leaning against the mantelpiece, looking down upon her with an expression of pain and tenderness. Something in his tone stirred Stasie's heart, and as she met his eyes she raised her head and exclaimed with animation—

"I believe you can cure me! No one else seems to understand *how* ill I am, not even I myself!"

"How can it be otherwise?" returned Brooke, mastering his agitation, and compelling himself to speak calmly, while he moved nearer, and bending one knee on a footstool before her, took both her hands gently between his own. "How can it be otherwise, when my life is bound up in yours? Yes! Stasie, I can save you, if you will give me the right to watch over you night and day, a right with which none can interfere!"

Stasie was silent from astonishment — astonishment so great that it had no room for shyness or embarrassment. She left her hands unresistingly in his, and his clasp 'grew closer as he went on. "I do not dare to suppose that you love me, but if—if you are indifferent to others—if your heart is all your own—a love so strong as mine, must win yours! I entreat you, do not reject me! my life has been one agony of fear, and, scarcely hope, since I come down here, anticipating this moment! look into my eyes, Stasie! and read more than my lips can tell!"

His whole aspect indeed attested the truth of his expressions; the veins on his somewhat rugged temples showed themselves, as if swollen by the quick tide of feverish circulation; the hands that grasped Stasie's shook slightly.

She was overwhelmed by the sight of a man ordinarily so calm, so self-controlled, to whom she looked up as to something above the common, thus overmastered by his emotion, and all for her! Still surprise was her strongest impression, only a subtile delightful glow of pride and joy and tenderness began to spread itself through her heart.

"And you feel all this for me ?" she exclaimed at length in a low soft tone, looking straight into his eyes with her honest earnest glance for a second, before it drooped and turned away. " Why do you care for me so much ?"

" How is it possible to explain the attraction one nature has for another ?" Brooke returned, a sense of hope, of possible success sending new fire along his veins. " I might tell you that you are fair and sweet enough to be the desire of any man's heart ; but you are more than this to me ! I have no hope, no ambition, no future unconnected with you in my heart, and with me, Stasie, you will regain your glorious health, your full power of enjoyment ; speak to me, Stasie ?"

She had gently withdrawn her hands, and held them clasped upon her knee. " I do not love you now," she said slowly, and raising her eyes to his again. " I did not think you cared for *me*. But if, oh ! if you love me so much, I *will* love you—love you well !" She held out her hands to him with an inexpressibly noble frank gesture of acceptance. Brooke kissed them with passionate delight, but felt he was only half through his difficulties.

" Then, Stasie, I have your promise that you will be my wife ? and that soon—very soon ? "

" Why so very soon ? " she asked, withdrawing her hands again, while he rose and sat down beside her. " I think an engagement must be very pleasant, people get to know each other. Ella Mathews and Mr. Baldwin used to be very happy, and——"

" But, dearest, I do not think we are bound to arrange our plans on the lines laid down by Mr. and Mrs. Baldwin," interrupted Brooke, who watched with eager satisfaction the brighter look, the healthier colour, that had come into her eyes and cheek. " You are very differently situated. You have no real home, and I may have to return to India. Shall you object to going to India ? "

" No," with a smile and quick soft blush, " though I am not so fond of Eastern things and people as I used to be."

" Ah ! you feel you have an enemy in that villain Kharapet ? "

Stasie hesitated a moment, and her lip quivered. " I am foolish, perhaps, but I *do* fear him. I cannot tell why ;" and, unconsciously, she drew a little nearer to Brooke.

"My darling," he cried, unable longer to resist his intense longing to hold her in his arms, though half afraid of startling her, he drew her gently to him, till her cheek lay against his heart.

"It is a true instinct! Hear me. I have reason to know that we must expect strong opposition from every one. From Mr. Harding because he does not wish you to marry any one for years to come; from Kharapet because you have rejected him (dog! that he should dare to raise his eyes to you), and because he is brewing devilish plots; from your guardian, because the others will influence him; from every one."

"From Mrs. Harding?" asked Stasie, strangely tempted to stay where she was and feel the strong throbbing of his heart, which made her own beat in sympathy.

"Mrs. Harding? oh, no. In her I have my best friend. I know I have her best wishes for my success with you. But I must speak plainly, Stasie; everything depends on our keeping our engagement profoundly secret for a short time."

"Why?" asked Stasie with natural surprise, and disengaging herself from him; "why should they object to you? you are as much a gentleman as I am a lady; indeed I daresay you are better born. They can only worry a little, which will not signify much."

"Ah, Stasie! I am aware I am no great match; as far as worldly advantages go, you might do much better than marry me; but I cannot be unselfish where you are concerned."

Stasie smiled an arch sweet smile. "I so hate having to conceal anything."

Brooke felt he was getting into the thick of it. He rose and walked once up and down the room, then reseating himself by her, he said gravely, "You say, dear, you will trust your future life to me. Is it too much then to be guided by me in our preliminary action? can you not believe that I have good and sufficient reasons for what I suggest? reasons which, when I explain them to you hereafter, you will acknowledge were *all*-sufficient. Can you have faith enough in me for this?"

"Yes, I can," said Stasie thoughtfully; "but I am puzzled."

"I am going to put your confidence in me to a still severer test," said Brooke, watching her countenance anxiously, and urged by an irresistible prompting from within to risk all in this first momentous interview.

"What is it?" asked Stasie nervously.

"I want you," said Brooke, speaking very low and distinctly, "I want you not only to keep our engagement secret, but to marry me soon, in about three weeks or so—privately—unknown to any one, and to come away with me somewhere until we are discovered, which of course we shall be before long; then no one can separate us, for you know the difficulties which surround the marriage of a minor are great."

"You ask me to run away with you," exclaimed Stasie, colouring to the roots of her hair, even down to where the lace wrapped her creamy throat. "To deceive Aunt Clem, who is so kind, and Mrs. Harding, and—— *You* propose this. I can scarce believe it. It is too extraordinary; you must have some reason, some very powerful reason; tell me what it is?"

"I have an all-powerful reason," returned Brooke; "one that you will acknowledge is sufficient, but I do not wish to tell it to you now."

"You must, you ought," said Stasie very

gravely. "You ask me to take a terrible step, and I believe in you so much that I feel sure you have some reason that seems good to you, but," hesitating a little, and timidly, "*I* may not think so, and indeed you must tell me."

"You have every right to ask, dearest," leaning his arm on the back of the sofa so as to draw nearer to her, and feeling that the tug of war had come. "It is most natural that such a proposition should raise the gravest doubts in your mind. I can but implore you to trust me : my conscience acquits me of any intention that is not blameless. Passionately as I love you, it is not the impatience of a lover that induces me to urge you to what you justly call a terrible step, but the forethought, the anxious care of a friend who would save you from—well, serious inconvenience. Will you not trust me, Stasie ? "

She looked at him searchingly, then covering her face with her hands, exclaimed, " It would be too shameful, before you have even asked my guardian's consent, which he *might* give. Oh ! I do trust you ; but there are some things of which none but one's own self can judge, and this is one. If I could speak to Mrs. Harding ! "

"Have you more confidence in her than in me?" asked Brooke, more as a special pleader than from any movement of jealousy; he had quite expected this resistance, distressing as it was. Stasie was not the kind of girl to be carried away by the first impassioned words of a lover. She was silent. "Have you more confidence in her?" repeated Brooke.

"Yes, in this matter; she is a woman," said Stasie slowly.

"I would gladly consult and confide in Mrs. Harding," resumed Brooke, but that I fear to expose her to her husband's brutal bad temper; and I am convinced that if I did tell her all, she would be on my side."

"No, we must not get her into a scrape," returned Stasie.

Brooke pleaded long and earnestly; he succeeded in making a certain impression, in creating serious uneasiness in Stasie's mind. She was not angry with him for what seemed to her so strange, so daring a proposition, but she could not conquer her repugnance to it. It was this shrinking from what seemed bold and indelicate, more than any distrust of him, that held her back.

Indeed, she had always looked up to him as the embodiment of all that was high-minded and cultivated, and the sudden revelation of his passionate love for herself, his strong emotion, his extreme tenderness, had shaken her mental equilibrium, and set her pulses throbbing with a fearful delight; but she did not lose her head so completely as to be blind to the reality of such a step as Brooke urged her to take, nor was she anxious to rush into marriage. A pleasant interval of companionship, time to know each other, to grow familiar, seemed to her desirable, as it is to most thoughtful girls. She felt too that he had gained immense sudden influence over her by the irresistible conviction of his great earnestness, which every word and look conveyed, and she half feared to yield to it.

Brooke too had patience with the scruples he respected, yet even his self-control began to fray out. She might trust him, she was a trifle too prudent, and time was so precious. He was almost tempted to tell her the truth, but a double fear held him back—first, lest he should seem wanting in coolness of judgment, and so be lowered in her estimation, should she disbelieve his theory of Kharapet's designs; secondly, if she accepted it, the strain on her sorely-tried nerves might be terribly injurious.

Finally Stasie, much moved by the look of despondency, almost despair, in Brooke's eyes, proposed to think over his proposition and give him a decided answer to-morrow.

"It will not be easy to see you alone," he said dejectedly.

"I can go and see Mrs. Harding, and—and you might be there and walk back with me," suggested Stasie, looking down.

"I have no doubt I shall manage it," said Brooke, smiling; "but we must be very cautious for the present. One promise you will give me, dearest; do not let this day's post pass without writing to your friend Mrs. Mathews; ask her to invite you as soon as possible. Nothing will do you so much good as change of air; besides, if you yield to my most ardent prayer, it will suit my plans to have you away from Sefton Park."

Stasie promised readily, and after a little more conversation, which, however, was slightly chilled by the difference between them, Brooke rose.

" I suppose I must go. Bhoodhoo, and even the amiable Mary, will report the unconscionable length of my visit. And Stasie, my own darling (you are my own, are you not?), you will try to bring your mind to what I ask. You do not doubt that I think of you more than of myself?"

" I do not indeed; but—do—*do* tell me why you ask such an extraordinary proof of my trust."

"Not now, I must not. Good-bye. I may come in this afternoon, I suppose, when Mrs. Harding is here. I could not stay away," kissing her hands, and then looking imploringly at her.

" I dare say you may," stepping back shyly.

There was a pause; Brooke half turned to go, then, springing to her side, he suddenly caught her in his arms and strained her to his heart. " By heaven! Stasie," he exclaimed in deep hurried tones of passionate entreaty, impressive resolve, " I cannot leave you. I will not let you go until you promise, solemnly promise to do exactly as I desire in this matter. My love! my life! you do not know what depends on your decision. I only seek your welfare, your safety." He held her close, looking down into her eyes.

A strange thrill of conviction quivered through Stasie's heart. Brooke had some knowledge she did not possess.

"You fear something," she exclaimed, clinging to him. "You fear, like me, you do not know what; you fear *for* me ? "

" I do, and I *know* what I fear." Stasie grew very pale, her lips quivered, her slender fingers clutched his arm.

" I will go with you," she whispered. "You are not easily frightened; it *is* something real. I have had strange thoughts sometimes, and life is very sweet."

"It is," he exclaimed; " and it shall be sweet to you, if it is in the power of man to make it so. You will then consent to a private marriage as soon as it can possibly take place ? you will be guided by me in all things ? "

" I will," returned Stasie, trembling as she leant against him. " I wish I could go away now. Could I not live with Mrs. Mathews till you get my guardian's consent ? "

" You will be better, safer with me, darling,"

cried Brooke, overjoyed at this sudden solution of his great difficulty.

"I should like to go away before Hormuz comes back. He hates me, I know he hates me. He will not come back for a few days."

"Then you can very well manage it. Write to Mrs. Mathews now, this moment—I will post the letter—you can have a reply the day after to-morrow, and start the following day."

Stasie at once sat down to her writing-table and rapidly traced a few lines, expressing her great need of change, and begging leave to come to her friends at once.

Brooke stood at a little distance, watching her with deepest delight, hardly able to believe that the moment of deliverance was at hand. Her fears were all directed to Kharapet; she did not seem to doubt Bhoodhoo; so much the better, she would be at rest comparatively. And after the emphatic warning Brooke had overheard Kharapet address to his tool, the latter would not attempt much for the next few days, after which danger would be at an end.

"Will that do?" said Stasie, handing him

her letter, with a simple confidence which touched him. Brooke glanced through it.

"It will do perfectly, seal it up and I will take it away at once. And now, my own! my love! you must give me one kiss, just one before I go, and say 'Jim, I love you.'"

Stasie hesitated; her sweet mouth quivered, she stretched out her arms, and with a burst of tears exclaimed, "I love you, Jim, for loving me so much!"

. . . . .

When she recovered herself a little she was strangely reluctant to be left alone. "I wish you could stay," she said.

"So do I," returned Brooke. "Suppose you come out with me; I will walk with you to Sefton House, and then go on to the post."

Stasie gladly accepted the proposition. She was thoroughly unhinged; the vague fear and dislike she had conceived of Kharapet had suddenly suggested the solution of Brooke's extraordinary and passionately-expressed desire that she should consent to a secret marriage and escape with him—from what, if not from some dreadful design of Kharapet's? The idea that a man so rational, so experienced as Brooke, should be ready to act on what *she* resisted as a morbid fancy, alarmed her profoundly. He *must* know more than he chose to say. She was well aware that Kharapet had great influence on Mr. Harding, and was all potent with her aunt. No one distrusted him save herself and Mrs. Harding; she felt therefore in some measure in his power.

What a strange, disturbed, anxious, thrilling day it had been! thought Stasie, when at an unusually early hour she escaped to her room. The sudden revelation of Brooke's love for her was bewildering, yet how her heart had leaped to answer his call upon it! She was half frightened to think how utterly, completely, she was his. To look back a few months, which seemed to have flown so fast, and which yet for her had been a whole cycle of life, and recall that first vision of him at Lady Elizabeth's *conversazione*, when she wondered who he could be, putting him down in her own mind as proud, cold, stern, and to-day he had trembled at her touch, and humbly begged for an assurance of her love. Again and again she lived over the strange experience of being folded in his arms, and wondered at the sense of safety, of delight, his embrace had given her. She would never feel at rest until Brooke had the right to stand between her and her enemy, if indeed Kharapet *was* the bitter enemy that from time to time she fancied him to be. This she had often doubted, but now that Brooke was evidently of the same opinion, she was convinced that the dim fancies which had agitated her were shadows of a reality.

Yet the idea of marrying under such circumstances tormented her; what would Mrs. Harding think? what would Aunt Clem say? How could she ever convey to them the hunted, terrified feeling, which made her ready to take refuge with Brooke, the only creature who seemed to perceive her need of help and protection? No matter, life was sweet; how sweet it would be with him! She would risk everything and be guided by his counsels.

CHAPTER XI.

THAT evening, while Stasie communed with her own heart, and Aunt Clem poured out to the sympathetic Susan her fears that her dear niece was far from strong—"She looked perfectly worn out, and I am sure the sooner she is away from this place the better," etc. etc.—Brooke was busy writing at one table, and his friend Robinson at another, with notes, letters, memoranda scattered about. "Robby," said the former looking up suddenly, "I must leave you in a few days. I shall have to go over to Paris, and I have matters to arrange previously in town."

"This is very sudden," cried Robinson, pausing, pen in hand. "I am very sorry; I shall miss you very much, old fellow! What is taking you away?"

"Business," returned Brooke briefly.

"I ought to ask why you stayed rather than why you leave," continued Robinson, nibbling the top of his pen. "I must say I have wondered why you came here."

"Your modesty, Robby! Don't you know I wanted to enjoy your society?"

"Well, joking apart, it has been a treat to me, and the place will be awfully dull when you go."

"I don't think I have been a particularly lively companion," returned Brooke, smiling grimly.

"Even so," replied Robinson with friendly candour. "It is not good for man to live alone."

"Oh! you have quite come to that conclusion?"

"Yes!" said Mr. Robinson, blushing. "It is, I believe, a very distinct injunction."

"To all, priests included?" asked Brooke.

"After mature reflection, I am convinced it is especially needful that priests should set an example of family life," said the young incumbent. Brooke smiled, indulgently this time, and resumed his writing; then after a few minutes' silence, "I think I shall stay in town for a few nights and go on to Paris next week."

" And then ? "

"Oh, I shall ultimately return to London."

"Mrs. Harding will miss you," said Robinson with a glance at his friend.

"Yes, I daresay," replied Brooke carelessly.

Little more passed between them that evening. Brooke was up at cock-crow next morning, and infinitely to the disgust of Mrs. Harris (who had formed a high opinion of her young master's stately, silent, but civil guest), departed for town before breakfast could be prepared. There's just one thing I can't abide; it's to see any one go out on an empty stomach," she grumbled to Mr. Robinson as that gentleman sipped his coffee an hour after. " It's just preparing one's self for fever and blood-poisoning, and everything that's bad."

.   .   .   .   .

Arrived in London, after a hasty breakfast at his club and a visit to his lodgings, where he occupied himself with a rearrangement of his baggage, Brooke sallied forth and walked quietly down Piccadilly. Near the circus he was stopped by a young man in civilian dress, but of

soldierly carriage, who exclaimed " Brooke ! I
fancied you were in Scotland ! at least they
thought so at the club ! I wanted to look you
up directly I came to town. Where have you
been ? "

" Ah, Thornton ! when did you arrive ? "

" About ten days ago. I have made a trading voyage of it home. My people were at
Florence ; then we went into the Tyrol for the
summer, had a peep at Vienna, up the Danube to
Passau, etc., and now I have run over here for a
week or two on business, and return to Paris the
day after to-morrow."

After some exchange of question and answer
respecting their mutual friends (the young man
was a captain in Brooke's regiment), Thornton
seemed disposed to attach himself to his newly-
discovered acquaintance, but Brooke soon disposed of him. " Sorry I am particularly
engaged to-day and to-morrow, my dear fellow !
but give me your address in Paris. I may be
there next month."

" You'll be sure to call," said Thornton, writing on the back of one of his cards; " my mother
will be delighted to see you."

Brooke thanked him, put the card carefully in his pocket-book, and, hailing a hansom, ordered the driver to Dalston, somewhat to the surprise of his friend, who stood on the kerb to see him drive off.

"The journey," almost "due north" was long and tedious, affording ample time to the traveller to meditate and arrange a somewhat complicated scheme, by which he hoped to steal a march on the enemy, and secure at least a fortnight of undisturbed happiness with his bride! It was almost incredible that he had cleared the difficulties, before which his spirit had quailed, at a bound. Stasie's curious instinctive dread of Kharapet had befriended him marvellously. But for that sudden revelation, that unexpected lifting of the cloud of hesitation and distrust by the pale spectre of terror, he could never have persuaded her against her better judgment; but now he felt sure of her, and his heart throbbed with pride and joy as the idea suggested itself, that she loved him better than she was herself aware!

But he resisted the tendency to dwell upon these delicious reminiscences, and set himself to think out steadily the details of his plan. His first care must be to lull suspicion as regarded himself. He must seem to leave London so soon as he was sure the day was fixed for Stasie's departure, and he must be resident for two or three weeks in any parish where his marriage was to take place ; round these leading lines the whole scheme must form itself. He had no particular business, nothing on hands that necessitated the forwarding of letters ; he might safely lose himself, and he could think of no more remote or unexplored region than that towards which he was now travelling. He never had known any one who had visited it, or come from it, and he only knew the name from seeing it on the map of London, or in the Registrar-General's report. There, at least, he could find obscurity, safety, and happiness. " Here we are, sir, where to now?" said the driver looking down through the trap-door at the top.

" Whereabouts is the parish church ? " was the counter-question.

" Don't know, sir. These parts is strange to me."

" Draw up. I'll ask myself."

Cabby obeyed. Brooke descended to make inquiries at a large grocery establishment. "The old parish church, sir?" said a stout, important-looking man, in a white apron, coming forward, as he noticed the boy behind the counter hesitate in his reply. "Why, it's more than two mile farther on."

"Then, may I ask, what is the nearest church—where you attend yourself?"

"Oh, *I* go to Mr. Sims', the Congregational Chapel in Hill's Place, sir; but there is a big church, St. Barnabas, about twenty minutes' walk from this, where there is an excellent preacher, the reverend Mr. Philips."

"Oh, indeed! and is it much attended? It is a district church, I suppose?"

"It is, sir."

"I suppose they have christenings, and marriages, and funerals there?"

"Plenty of marriages and christenings, sir. The funerals are conducted in the cemetery."

"Thank you! I am very much obliged. Pray, which is the way to this church?"

"Drive straight down this street to the end, where there is a broad road crossing it, turn left, and then take the second to the right ; you will see the church before you."

Brooke thanked him courteously, and, leaving the shop, conveyed these directions to Jehu ; then, jumping in, they drove off smartly.

" I wonder what that tall grand-looking chap is after ? " said the jovial master of the establishment. " Has he a baby to christen, or a parent to bury ? "

" Maybe he has a young lady to marry on the sly ? " suggested the elder assistant. " He looks a reg'lar west-end swell." The master and his men chuckled over the notion, and business resumed its sway.

Meantime Brooke's conveyance stopped before the church, and Brooke, descending, asked, " How much ? "

" Six-and-six, sir. It's a long stretch," said the driver tentatively. Brooke paid without a question, being averse to impress himself on the man's memory. " Thank'ee, sir." Brooke left him rather ostentatiously rubbing his horse's head and neck, as if the animal had been over-driven, and strolled round the handsome edifice, which was environed by a border of grass, with posts and chains. A semicircle of new houses, of a higher class than those in the neighbourhood, partially surrounded it ; Brooke noticed on one of them the inscription " St. Barnabas Parsonage ;" then, after standing for a moment in deep thought, he turned briskly down one of the streets leading from " Granville Crescent," as the semicircle was named, and walked briskly for a few minutes, looking sharply right to left, as he went, at the houses.

He was seeking for lodgings, and seemed very hard to please, when he found a locality where frequent announcements of " apartments " adorned the windows.

He scemed more interested in the landladies than their rooms ; some of scrupulous cleanliness and neatness rather took his fancy ; but when the mistress of the house appeared severe, metallic, unbending, or dressy, smiling, and over-gracious, he declined to decide, and retreated rapidly. He had thus visited five or six abodes —all, as their owners declared, perfect in their appointments, their order, their freedom from noxious insects, etc., and still he was unsuited. He was, in truth, anxious respecting the aspect of the landlady, for he knew that he should be obliged to place Stasie alone in whatever rooms he chose, for at least part of a day and a night, and he was keenly alive to the unavoidable pain and discomfort she must endure even under the most favourable arrangements. He, therefore, sought eagerly for a motherly respectable-looking hostess, who could be some stay to his *fiancée*. How shameful, how infamous, that she should be obliged to save her life at the cost of such concealment!

But time was pressing; he wanted to be at Limeville that afternoon, and he must engage a lodging before he returned.

At length he reached a neat row of semi-detached villas with gardens, and in the window of one he discovered an *affiche*.

"You have rooms to let?" he asked, as the door was opened by a diminutive but tidy servant.

"Yes, sir; walk in, please, and I'll call missis." Brooke was beginning to be tired and impatient of the oft-repeated formula. Immediately, from some region below, arose a stout, fresh, kindly-looking, brown-eyed person, not quite a lady, but above the average letter of lodgings. She was very neatly dressed in a clean print and a black apron. With pleasant courtesy she showed Brooke a bright, if somewhat gaudy parlour, lighted by a bay-window, and a fairly comfortable bedroom behind it. Brooke paused in deep thought as she named a moderate price enough for the accommodation, and the good woman, fancying he hesitated at the terms, observed, "Of course, sir, if it were for a permanency that would make a difference."

"It will not be for more than three weeks or a month," said Brooke, rousing himself. "May I ask if you have any children?"

"Not young children, sir. I have two girls; one goes to school, and the eldest is daily governess in a family close by."

That sounded well. Brooke liked the aspect of the house and its owner. "I will take your rooms," he said, "from the day after to-morrow."

"Very well," with a little hesitation; "but I have been advised always to ask for references."

"A necessary precaution," said Brooke, with a smile. "There is my card. I will write the address of my agents, Messrs. Grindlay, on the back, they will answer for me ; but as I am a total stranger to you I will pay a week's rent in advance," taking out his purse. "I shall, probably, not come in till Monday next, but I am your tenant from Saturday."

"Well, sir, I can have no objection as you are so straightforward ; sit down for a minute or two till I write a receipt."

But Brooke was too restless and excited to rest quiet—he paced the room. He congratulated himself on its cheerful outlook, as a street opening in front showed a glimpse of the church. He pictured to himself Stasie's embarrassment and trepidation at arriving there alone. It would be a tremendous trial for her, yet he could not help a thrill of delight at the idea of consoling and encouraging her. While he thought thus he heard the door open, and turning met a very pretty, dark-eyed, ladylike girl face to face; she was well and quietly dressed in outdoor attire. "I beg your pardon," blushing, "I thought my mother was here."

Brooke made her a low bow, and she went quickly away. "The very place," he murmured.

His new landlady soon returned, smiling and

contented. "Here is the receipt, sir, and my card, and what would you like for dinner, sir, on Monday? and what hour are you likely to come in?"

"I will write you all particulars," said Brooke, putting away the receipt and card, on which was printed, "Mrs. Hicks, 9 Alma Villas, Dalston," carefully in a breast pocket, "and now I must bid you good-morning."

"And I trust you will find yourself comfortable in my house, sir."

"I have no doubt I shall."

Brooke, observing it was not a neighbourhood where cabs were to be found, asked his way to the nearest omnibus line, and walked off rapidly.

. . . . .

Aunt Clem had been only partially successful in her house-hunting, and Stasie was too much upset, too visibly unwell, to hear any description of the chase on her return.

Next morning, however, our heroine woke up wonderfully refreshed and strengthened. Her first thought was that she had given her solemn promise to Brooke, and that in a sense she belonged to him—a thought that had less of fear and more of joy than it possessed yesterday. She was also less impressed by her own vague terror of Kharapet, but deeply convinced that Brooke knew something very important, very inimical to her own welfare, or he would never urge her to so desperate a step as an elopement! She could scarce bear to think of it. How ardently she longed to see Brooke's face, to hear his voice; nothing else could give her courage. But he had told her he would not be with her till the afternoon, so Stasie composed herself to listen attentively to her aunt, towards whom her heart swelled with repentant tenderness, as she thought what a state the poor lady would be in when she found herself deserted and deceived.

"You must be so tired, auntie, after your long day yesterday," she said kindly, putting a footstool under Miss Stretton's feet.

"Yes, my dear, I am; but the worst was to find you looking like a ghost when I came back. You are quite a different being this morning. Were you too much by yourself?"

"Oh, no; Dr. Brooke," turning to fetch her work-basket, "came in; he expected to find Mrs.

Harding here; and then I went to see Mademoiselle Aubert, and walked with her and the children; then Mrs. Harding came back. It does me so much good to go out. Now tell me all you did."

"Well, my love, if there is anything more exhausting than another, it is looking for houses; going up and downstairs, and being worried with the caretakers, who always try and put you against the place. I saw very nice apartments in Upper Baker Street that would suit perfectly well, and we might just keep Mary as a ladies' maid; but Mr. Kharapet is dead against apartments; he thinks you ought to have a house of your own now."

"Don't mind him, auntie; just choose what you like."

"Rather what you like, my dear! I cannot decide on anything without you."

"I am sure you may. I shall like whatever you choose."

"It is very sweet of you to say so, dear. But don't you think we should be quite comfortable in lodgings?"

"Yes," thoughtfully; "only I should not like

to send away Bhoodhoo, poor fellow : what would become of him ? "

" Well, Stasie, we really cannot arrange our plans merely to provide for Bhoodhoo."

" Perhaps not."

" It is all very well to be so very considerate for others, but there is a duty," etc. etc. Stasie heard the murmur of her aunt's refined and somewhat monotonous voice, but, deep in her own thoughts, lost all consciousness of what she was saying, till roused by the cessation of sound.

" Ah, auntie, how I wish I were of age ! "

" Why, Stasie ? " in some surprise.

" Oh ! I should like to give you some money, what they call settle it upon you, or leave it to you in my will, so that you should never be obliged to live in a miserable patched-up bedroom again."

" My dear child ! my sweet Stasie ! " rising to kiss her, and then resuming her seat. " You are kind and thoughtful beyond your years : I am deeply touched by your affectionate care. Do not trouble about me, my love ! The Lord will provide ; and in any case that good kind Mr. Kharapet would be a true friend."

"Do you think Hormuz would do anything for you? or give you a farthing of my money if I were gone? for all mine would be his. You little know him. Why, Aunt Clem, don't you see he is a mass of spite and selfishness? He hates me, and——"

"Stasie, Stasie! You must have lost your senses to talk in this way of your best friend! You used to be quite fond of him," cried Miss Stretton, aghast at such unholy sentiments.

"Friend!" cried Stasie, bursting into tears. "I have not a real friend in the world but you and Mrs. Harding. Even Mrs. Mathews does not care for me as much as she used!"

"My darling child! You are not at all yourself! You are weak and low. Do have a little sal volatile or camphor, or—dear me—I was in hopes you were ever so much better this morning! Do let me send for Dr. Hunter."

"No, no, no," said Stasie, trying to recover herself. "He could do nothing. I am only weak and stupid. I am so sure nothing will do me good but change that I wrote yesterday to Mrs. Mathews asking leave to go down to her for a week or two."

"Very right, dear," cried Miss Stretton, too startled and uneasy to object to anything. "I am sure it will do you good ; and if she cannot take you in we will just pack up and go to Aix-les-Bains or—or—Cannes, or Mentone—or anywhere. Why should you be moped to death here for any one's fancies ? You may count on me, my dear, dear Stasie ! I will submit to any sacrifice for your sake !"

Embraces and tears ensued, and Stasie, glancing at the clock, saw to her delight that the hand pointed to three.

"I think I will go and ask Mrs. Harding to walk with me," said Stasie restlessly. She felt as if she could not meet Brooke in her aunt's presence, and that he would be sure to follow her to Sefton House.

"Very well, dear ! I daresay you will find Dr. Brooke there. I fancy he is there most of his time."

"Not more than he is here," replied Stasie, unable to let this pass.

"Perhaps not ! Mrs. Harding is here nearly as much as in her own house."

"Aunt," said Stasie, colouring crimson. "I

am sure you are quite mistaken. I do not believe Dr. Brooke thinks of his cousin as——in the way you imagine!"

"Well, then, what makes him stay down here? I am sure I hope you are right. I can't help liking him, in spite of the rude way Mr. Kharapet heard him speak of me; and he has been looking wretchedly ill, poor man!"

"I am certain he never spoke rudely of you, auntie! I don't care what Mr. Kharapet said he heard, I am certain Dr. Brooke never did."

With this parting shot Stasie walked out of the room, leaving Aunt Clem bewildered, with a sensation as though the earth had opened up before her, and there was no longer a firm foothold to be found anywhere.

Putting on her hat occupied Stasie longer than usual, and when she returned to the drawing-room she found her aunt ensconced in an easy-chair, in conversation with Brooke, who was standing on the hearth-rug. Fortunately Miss Stretton's back was to the door, so she did not see Stasie's sudden vivid blush, her change of expression, as her eyes fell upon the visitor. Her heart fluttered for a moment with a wild thrill, half joy, half fear.

"Going out, Miss Verner?" asked Brooke advancing to meet her, with what she thought marvellous coolness and composure; but so soon as her hand was in his she recognised how thin was the seeming, when, feeling that he intervened between Miss Stretton and her niece, he laid his other hand over hers in a mute caress.

"Yes," replied Stasie, a little unsteadily. "I am going to see Mrs. Harding!"

"Indeed! May I come with you? I find I shall have to go to Paris the beginning of next week, and I want to tell her my plans."

"Very well," said Stasie, still trembling with a strange faintness. "I will take Pearl; the children like to see him."

"My love to Mrs. Harding. I am much too tired to go out to-day," said Miss Stretton amiably.

"I want you to take a long walk with me, Stasie. I want to talk to you of a hundred things, and it seems years since I saw you yesterday," said Brooke, as soon as they were clear of the house.

"And I want to talk with you so much," replied Stasie. "I have been miserable—no, not altogether miserable, but so restless and frightened. But I must ask Mrs. Harding to come with us."

"Very well," returned Brooke, after a moment's hesitation, and kept silence till the short distance was accomplished.

Mrs. Harding was at home, and the children soon carried off Pearl to their special garden. Then Brooke told his cousin he was going over to Paris the following week for a short visit, and that he would not probably return to Sefton Park. "Indeed, you will all be flown by that time. I shall find you in town, eh, Livy?"

"Yes. We will move about the twentieth of next month."

Then Stasie, a little timidly, asked Mrs. Harding if she would come out. Brooke, at whom Mrs. Harding glanced (feeling in some inexplicable instinctive way that he and Stasie understood each other), slightly shook his head, and Mrs. Harding answered quietly, "No, dear; I have a good deal to do to-day."

"There is not much time," remarked Brooke to Stasie. "The evenings close in so soon."

Then Stasie found herself walking away down the avenue of elms, and soon turned into a path which led through a strip of woodland to the highroad.

"We are tolerably safe here," said Brooke, drawing her hand through his arm. "Now, let us talk over everything, for we shall probably not have another opportunity."

How long the memory of that day dwelt in Stasie's heart!—the crisp rustle of the withered leaves, the subtile perfume of the larch and pine-trees, the single note uttered at intervals by some bird not quite resigned to coming winter, the murmur of a little brook that prattled along its pebbly course near the path, as they walked to and fro beneath the sheltering trees; and Stasie felt all doubt and fear and hesitation melt away as she listened to Brooke's clear, decided statement of his well-defined plan, or wondered at the amazing change in him from the cool, rather indifferent man of the world, to the eager, tender lover, whose controlled ardour testified to his care and consideration for her. He seemed to be years younger than when she first met him—blither, softer, more genial.

"It is quite dusk," said Stasie at length. "I must not stay any longer." She was growing more at home with him, more deliciously familiar. "And there is one thing I should like to say to you, only I am half afraid——"

"Tell me everything," interrupted Brooke; "every thought of your heart. You have no choice, my own darling, but to trust me in all things."

"Don't you think, then," resumed Stasie, coming a little closer, "that we might manage to wait, if I stayed with Mrs. Mathews, until you could get Mr. Wyatt's consent? I might refuse to leave—I can be very determined—and—— Oh! it is not that I doubt you, but I do shrink from a marriage of this kind, it seems so terrible. Is it not possible to manage in some other way?"

"Stasie, it is *not* possible!" returned Brooke impressively. "Believe me, *you* do not wish to avoid such an alternative more than I do. I would wait willingly for you, dearest, for months, rather than hurry you into such an undertaking, were it not that I feel convinced you will be safe only when you are my wife. Keep this before your mind, and let no hesitation disturb you. Have confidence in me : can you not believe that your safety, your welfare, are paramount with me ?"

"I can, I will," said Stasie, moved and convinced ; "only when—when everything is settled, I must do something to make Aunt Clem comfortable for life."

"You shall do what you like with your own, and I will help you."

"Ah ! yes, I want your help so much, and " —a wistful look into his eyes—"I do hope I shall get well and strong, and not trouble you with anxiety or sickliness."

"My love," drawing her to him with infinite tenderness, "you shall be well and strong, and we shall enjoy life together ; but if not, who can care for you and tend you as I will. I take you for better, for worse."

Tears sprang to Stasie's eyes as she unconsciously pressed close against him.

"I will see you home," said Brooke, "but we must part here," and clasping her in his arms he kissed her brow and eyes and lips, with more of passion than he had hitherto allowed himself to show.

CHAPTER XII.

THE following day brought a joint letter from
Mrs. Mathews and Ella. The former was greatly
vexed that she could not take in her dear Stasie.
Her house was already crammed, but Ella had a
nice spare room, which was quite at Stasie's service; and Ella herself wrote a most hearty and
loving invitation. Unfortunately she could not
receive her friend till the following Wednesday.

Stasie would have liked to start the very next
day. It was intolerable to her to be in hourly
communication with her aunt, who was more
than usually attentive and affectionate, and yet
to keep silent respecting the thoughts that filled
her brain to bursting, with joy and fear and hope
and pride.

Her only calm and happy moments were when
Brooke was present, then a subtile warmth and
strength seemed to fill her veins as with a potent

life-giving elixir, and she knew how her heart had elected him as its mate, its other self, from the first moment they had met, though she had mastered its natural cravings.

But Brooke was only occasionally at Sefton Park during the few succeeding days. He had gone back to stay in London, and the Rev. St. John Robinson was quite dull for want of his companionship. When Brooke did come, too, Stasie could rarely secure a few moments' private conversation with him. She never forgot the strange slowness, and yet awful rapidity, with which those intervening hours flitted away.

At length the last day but one was upon them; the last day but one before she would quit Mrs. Harding and Aunt Clem, never to return to them as Stasie Verner; for in spite of her repugnance to the course she was obliged to pursue, she felt it would be still more terrible if her marriage with Brooke were prevented.

Brooke came in rather late in the afternoon. He looked bright, alert—like a man on the road to success—and made himself especially agreeable to Miss Stretton, too much so, for she persisted in remaining gracefully posed in her easy-chair, till Brooke began to think he must ask Stasie to come out with him, which he did not like to do, as it was raining heavily. Still nothing else was left for it, and he had just opened his lips to broach the subject when enter Mary with a note, " If you please 'm, is there any answer ? "

" Wait a moment," hastily opening it. " I hope the messenger is not gone ? "

" No 'm."

" Then I shall just go and give him the answer myself. Stasie, dear, do you know where my receipt-book is ? "

" I believe it is locked up in your Davenport in the morning-room," said Stasie falteringly.

Aunt Clem left the room briskly.

" Thank God ! " ejaculated Brooke, starting up, and, coming over beside Stasie, took out his pocket-book, "tell me your address at C——, my darling, quick ; care of the Rev. G. Baldwin, The College, C—— " (writing quickly), " is that all ? Then Stasie, you shall find a letter from me on your arrival giving you *my* address—you might let it be seen were I to give it to you here, and *no* clue must be given. Write to me the moment you arrive : I shall know no peace till I hear you are safe with your friends. How awfully you tremble! courage, my own love! in some ten or twelve days we shall be safe away. One thing more, lend me one of your rings, you shall have it again." He had only time to kiss the hand that gave it, and conceal the ring, when Miss Stretton sailed in again.

"I am sure, Dr. Brooke, you will excuse me. Our neighbour, Mrs. Morison, wrote to beg the loan of my receipt-book. It was rather a liberty, but I could not refuse, and it was not in the Davenport, Stasie, it was on the mantelpiece."

"I only waited your return to make my adieux," said Brooke. "I have to say a word to Robinson, then I must catch the five train."

"Good-bye then, my dear sir. I trust you will enjoy your visit to bright, beautiful Paris."

"I have no doubt I shall," said Brooke significantly. "Have you any commands? The little Hardings have given me endless commissions. Good-bye, Miss Verner; remember my advice—hope, and plenty of exercise. I expect to see you looking much better when we meet again."

A close pressure of her hand, and he was gone.

"He is quite right, Stasie, my dear; you should not despond about yourself. I am sure a change to London will do all the good in the world."

"I think it will," said Stasie, smiling archly, though tears stood in her eyes; "and I earnestly hope I shall never give you any more trouble, auntie," kissing her. "Now I will go away and finish packing."

"Very well, dear! but you seem to me to be taking a great deal more than you will want."

"I do not not think so, Aunt Clem."

Meantime Brooke was exchanging a few last words with his old schoolfellow; they had shaken hands when Brooke exclaimed, "I had nearly forgotten, will you take charge of this parcel?" —it looked like a couple of books tied up in brown paper—"till I come back, or I will write to you about it."

"Certainly, with pleasure."

"Good-bye, old fellow! take take of yourself."

.   .   .   .   .

It was a gray lowering day when Stasie started for C——. She had felt faint and ill with the wild beating of her heart, which always filled her with uneasiness, the night before her departure. This greatly increased her intense desire to escape. A vague dim fear of poison was forming itself in her mind as the only solution of Brooke's hints and her own sensations; but she contrived to conceal her indisposition. Nothing, she was determined, should interfere with her journey.

Miss Stretton accompanied her to town. At Waterloo they were met by Kharapet, who escorted them to King's Cross, and was infinitely amiable, smooth, insinuating, yet Stasie shrank from him almost visibly. She read something sinister in his glance, something sneering and treacherous in his smile, nor did she breathe freely till the steam-whistle sounded, and she was whirled away from her old life for ever.

The quiet days, the rest, the sense of safety in Ella's simple happy home, were of infinite service in calming Stasie's excited nerves, and restoring tone to her spirits. At first Mrs. Mathews and her daughter were greatly distressed to see how pallid and worn she looked, to observe how readily her eyes filled with tears, and how violently she started at the least noise. Gradually these symptoms disappeared, and Stasie grew more like herself, though restless, always wishing to be out of doors, watching for the postman, and constantly writing letters, which she preferred to post herself.

"Believe me, Stasie has more in her head than you think," said Mrs. Mathews to her daughter. "I never saw a girl so changed—indeed, I must say, improved—she is so gentle and ready to hear reason, and thoughtful. I am certain she is in love."

"Oh, no, mother! she would be sure to tell me!"

"Don't you be too sure ; look how she watches the postman!"

Oh! the delight, the pride, the strength conveyed by those letters! It was worth being all that way away from *him* to have them! and how delicious, though puzzling, to reply, for Stasie never could bring herself to write honeyed phrases, but sought to veil her tenderness in playful conceits and saucy little quibbles, which sent many a thrill of joy through the heart of the reader as he noticed that her mind was regaining its tone.

On the whole a fortnight slipped away much faster than Stasie expected, and the moment of departure had come.

" I do wish, dear, you could have stayed just one week longer," said Ella, as she stood with her friend on the platform at the C—— station, whither Mrs. Mathews, Janet, and one of the younger boys had also come to speed the parting guest. " You are so very much better. You would have been *quite* yourself in a few days more."

" You have done me worlds of good indeed, but it would have been *quite* impossible for me to stay," returned Stasie, who was flushed and feverish. " I will write to you, dear, as soon as I get to town, just to say I am safe. You must really come and see me when we are settled in London."

Here the youngest Mathews boy came running up. " Here are your stamps, Stasie, and the change ; I posted the letter all right."

" Thank you, thank you. No, I don't want the change, keep it. Oh ! here is train. Good-bye, Ella. Good-bye, dear, dear Mrs. Mathews ; I can never, never forget all your goodness to me," embracing her with tears.

" My dear, there was little I could do for you. Are you sure your luggage was ticketed ? "

" Yes ! I saw to that," cried Fred, the third boy, proudly. " They'll go all right, but she never put her name on the box."

" Good-bye !   Be sure you write ! "

" Best regards to Mr. Baldwin ; thank him for all his kindness ;" and she was off.

" Tell me, Tom," said his mother, as they walked slowly towards home, " how was the letter addressed that you posted for Stasie ? "

" I dunno," said Tom. " I think there was Sefton Park on it."

" Sefton Park ! " repeated his mother ; " that is strange, when she is going straight back there ; it is very strange."

.   .   .   .   .

That lonely journey was probably Stasie's greatest trial, but there was ample compensation at the end of it, when Brooke, who had been on the watch for some time, opened the carriage door, and with a hasty whispered " At last, my darling, at last ! " assisted her to alight, and, drawing her hand through his arm, went to extricate her luggage. This was quickly accomplished, for the train was not crowded. Then Stasie felt as if all her troubles were over. She had in effect crossed the rubicon, and put herself beyond the region of doubt. She possessed that most precious gift that can bless the soul of woman, complete faith in the knowledge, wisdom, and honour of the man her heart prompted her to love, and she was with him now for ever.

At Alma Terrace a vigorous preparation had gone on since morning. Brooke, after a week's residence, had announced the object of his sojourn. His landlady and her daughter showed the warmest sympathy. Indeed Brooke always got on well with women, and though he said as little as he could possibly help in explanation of the privacy he wished to maintain, both mother and daughter united in constructing a little romance highly creditable to the fascinating doctor if not to " his young lady."

It can therefore be imagined how delighted Stasie was to be welcomed by a portly, kindly, respectable-looking woman, who received her with much deference and evident sympathy; then Brooke, laughing gaily, called for Miss

Hicks, and presenting her to his *fiancée*, said, " I flatter myself I have remembered most things, and I claim great credit in having provided you with a bridesmaid."

" Thank you, very much," said Stasie, whose colour went and came with natural emotion, penetrated as she was by the tender thought shown for her by her lover, and she held out her hand to the pleased smiling girl.

A bright fire, plenty of flowers, a table laid for dinner, gave a gala aspect to the sitting-room.   Mrs. Hicks was ready to act as a motherly lady's - maid, and the terrible sense of being ashamed of herself began to be lifted from poor Stasie's heart.

" Well, she is a sweet young lady," was the judgment pronounced on her downstairs.

" She is indeed, mother.   She is quite beautiful ; any gentleman might want to run away with her.   And isn't he fond of her ! He looks years younger than he did yesterday."

" I am sure I hope they'll be happy," returned the mother with a sigh.   " Now I have seen *both*, I am quite sure it must have been heartless brutes that came between them ! they seem just made for each other; but he is a good bit older than she is. I *am* glad I persuaded him to have a cake. I'm sure the young lady would have thought it a poor compliment not to have a cake! Here, 'Lisbeth, the fowl is done to a turn, get the tray quick. Love or no love, people must eat."

Upstairs, when Stasie had removed her wraps and smoothed her hair, and come back to the sitting-room with a slight graceful embarrassment, Brooke caught her hands in his, exclaiming, "Now let me have a good look at you after all these long weeks." There was nothing in the deep tender interest of his gaze to make it insupportable.

"I see you are nearly yourself again. My love! you have left all the ills, from which care and affection can shield you, behind, when you escaped that sneaking devil Kharapet."

The evening passed quickly in talking over their plans.

"Aunt Clem writes me word that she has taken a small house in Upper Baker Street," said Stasie after a short pause, "and I fancy from what she says that Mr. Harding and Hormuz

Kharapet have nearly quarrelled over it. Hormuz would not agree to our having apartments, and Mr. Harding thinks the house too dear. Oh, Jim! what a frightful row there will be when everything is found out!"

"I expect there will," returned Brooke philosophically: "but that will not matter much if we can keep out of the way for a fortnight or so, and I have had a letter posted for Robinson in Paris that will rather throw them off the scent."

"You will never let any one take me away from you, Jim?"

"I should like to see any one try," rather grimly. "Do you know, I have had to do a bit of hard swearing for you. When I applied for the license, the fellow in authority—surrogate I think—asked about your age, and the consent of parents, etc. I said you were an orphan; fortunately he did not press for particulars, and only warned me of the penalty I incurred if I married a minor against the consent of her protectors. I wish, Stasie, I could catch Wyatt before Harding and Kharapet get hold of him. But it is time for me to leave you; I want you to get a good night's rest. Good-night, my love, my own! this is our last parting." A long embrace, and, calling Mrs. Hicks, he enjoined upon her special care of the young lady before he went away to the hotel where he was to sleep.

The next morning they were married.

.   .   .   .   .

Meantime all went smoothly at Sefton Park. Mrs. Harding's removal to town had been delayed in consequence of Willie having taken a severe cold. Miss Stretton was briskly, cheerfully preparing for her own removal, highly pleased at the idea of being settled in town for the winter, and quite convinced by Kharapet's reasonings that a house and establishment of her own was much more suitable to Stasie's comfort and dignity than furnished lodgings. "The thought and consideration of that dear man is quite amazing," she observed to Mrs. Harding the afternoon of the day on which Stasie was married, as she walked with her towards Limeville, after a ramble through the rector's fields, all unconscious of the important event which had taken place that morning.

"He gives himself a good deal of trouble, and irritates Mr. Harding more than is necessary," replied his wife. " You would have been quite comfortable in furnished lodgings."

" Perhaps so ; but certainly a house is much more *comme il faut*. Ah! here is Mr. Robinson."

The incumbent raised his hat with his usual urbanity, and after an interchange of greetings, asked if Aunt Clem had good accounts of Miss Verner.

" Excellent, my dear sir ; she writes in good spirits, and intends to remain another week. She asked, in her sweet way, if I could spare her for a little longer as she was feeling so much better. Of course I told her to stay by all means, that I could manage our moving without her. This morning I had a few lines thanking me, and I imagine they are going to have company or something, for she says she will be much occupied, and that she will not write again this week."

" Very glad she is so much better, and very sorry we are to lose her and you, Miss Stretton."

" By the bye, have you heard anything of Dr. Brooke ? He has not written since he left," said Mrs. Harding.

" I had a note from him a few days ago from Paris, asking me to send some books he had left at my place to his old lodgings, and he desired his kind regards to you."

" Did he say when he was coming back ? "

" No ; there were not half-a-dozen lines in all."

" I daresay he may go on to Brussels. He has been wanting to see Brussels."

" He is a lucky fellow to be able to run about as he likes. Good morning ;" and Mr. Robinson passed on.

There was some cleaning and white-washing to be done in the house selected by Miss Stretton, or, rather, by Kharapet, and the workmen were, as usual, procrastinating and provoking, so the days went past, and Miss Stretton grew impatient and weary of living half-packed up, and far from comfortable.

" It is very wretched here," she said one afternoon more than a week after the above conversation, as she was parting from her friend Mr. Kharapet, who had been enjoying some of Bhoodhoo's best dishes, and bidding her adieu. I do wish you would call at the house-agent's and endeavour to hasten him. The Hardings will be away on Thursday, and I really cannot stay here alone."

"No; certainly not. We will hasten these lazy dogs. We will make our dear Stasie return to you."

"Indeed, I am astonished Stasie does not write, and, by the way, there was a letter for her this morning. I will send it on, and ask what she is about——"

"A letter for Stasie?" interrupted Kharapet, with sudden sharp curiosity. "Let me see it."

Miss Stretton obeyed. It was a ship letter, directed in a straggling hand, and the envelope was of the commonest. It was, moreover, addressed to Mr. Harding's care, and had been re-addressed by one of the clerks. Kharapet turned it over and over; his fingers itched to open it, but he dared not.

Returning it to Aunt Clem, he said gently, "Yes, dear lady, I would send it on at once, and beg her to fix a day for her return. I shall be here again the day after to-morrow, and hope to tell you that your new abode is ready. If you will write a few lines to Stasie I can post them in town."

Miss Stretton complied, and the Syrian carried off the epistle and its enclosure with him.

.　　.　　.　　.　　.

The next day but one Kharapet made his appearance at an unusually early hour. He wanted to consult Mr. Harding (who was not going into town that day) respecting some matter of business, and to return to the city before noon. But he found time enough to pause at Limeville, and give Bhoodhoo a private hint that he had not yet breakfasted.

He was so early that Miss Stretton had not appeared above the visible horizon. She was not an early riser either by taste or habit. Kharapet therefore waited with what patience he could. He tried to read the paper, but in vain; his attention was engrossed by two letters which lay on the breakfast-table, addressed to Miss Stretton, one in a curious, left-handed looking writing, while the other, a thick packet, had the C—— postmark.

Presently Miss Stretton, arrayed in a " sweet " morning-cap and smiling a gracious welcome, entered.

" How very kind of you, dear Mr. Kharapet,

to come in *sans cérémonie!* I hope Bhoodhoo
has something nice for us."

"You are always well provided," with a bow;
"but do not let me keep you from your letters,"
handing them to her.

"Dear me! whom can this be from?" examining the smaller envelope. "I seem to know the
hand, and yet I don't. 'N. E.,' I know no one
in the N. E. district; but this, this is Mrs. Baldwin's writing," tearing it open in haste, and letting
a letter fall out, whilst she glanced with changing
colour at a note enclosed.

"Oh, good gracious! What has become of
her? Oh, read, read, Mr. Kharapet! my head is
turning round."

Kharapet seized the paper with fierce eagerness, and read—

"DEAR MISS STRETTON—Janet says she is
sure the enclosed is from you. I therefore lose
no time in returning it. I trust there is nothing
wrong; but dear Stasie left us on the 28th, by
the 12.30 train for King's Cross.—Yours very
truly,   ELLA BALDWIN."

Kharapet uttered an exclamation in some unknown tongue, and then stood silent, paralysed.

Miss Stretton burst into tears. "My dear child, my precious niece! She has been robbed and murdered, and heaven only knows what."

"Bah!" broke out Kharapet furiously, for once natural and unrestrained. "Don't you see she is gone of her own free will. She has fled with some one, and escaped—escaped!"

"I don't believe it, I can't believe it," cried Aunt Clem.

"Read this!" he exclaimed, in a tone of rude command, and he tore the other letter open for her.

"Ah!" cried Aunt Clem, "it is from herself;" and she read—

"DEAR AUNT—I am well, safe, and happy.
—"STASIE."

"I don't believe it," sobbed Miss Stretton hysterically. "Some villain has forced her to write this with a pistol at her head!"

Kharapet did not heed her. He was closely examining the writing, the envelope, the signatures of both letters.

"*She* never would go away with any one," continued Miss Stretton. "She did not care enough for any one——"

"I must take these to Mr. Harding at once," interrupted Kharapet, who was greatly agitated, and even forgetful of his breakfast. "It is most mysterious. Hear me!" he said, harshly, roughly, to the weeping, trembling woman beside him, "Be silent in the matter. Do not let the household know. Should we discover and bring her back, their ignorance would make her return easier."

"I will not say a word," cried poor Aunt Clem, terrified and obedient. "But do wait for me. I will put on my bonnet in a moment. I can't stay here by myself."

"You can follow," returned Kharapet, in the same abrupt savage tone; and gathering up the letters he crushed them into his pocket. Miss Stretton hesitated an instant, and then followed him into the hall, where she found him speaking rapidly and emphatically in Hindoostanee to Bhoodhoo, whose big dark eyes were alight with an expression of surprise and alarm. Neither noticed her; and when Kharapet ceased to speak, Bhoodhoo said something in reply—a few words —but ending in "doctor Sahib," at which Kharapet shook his head, and, with an exclamation, went rapidly away.

CHAPTER XIII.

THE morning meal at Sefton House was over. Mr. Harding had thrown down his table-napkin and taken up the *Times*, the children had gone for their morning run before settling to lessons, and Mrs. Harding's hand was on the door, as she was going to her diurnal interview with " cook," when Kharapet, pale, breathless, rushed in, nearly overturning Mrs. Harding in his onset.

"She is gone, fled, we know not whither?" he gasped, his face greenly white, his eyes flashing angrily, viciously.

"Who has gone? what's the matter? are you out of your mind, man?" exclaimed Mr. Harding, rising.

"Stasie!" cried Mrs. Harding, with a stunned feeling, as if dazed by a sudden revelation.

"Ah! yes, Stasie. You knew, did you?" cried Kharapet, turning on her fiercely.

"I say, what the deuce is the matter?" said Harding, looking from one to the other, half angry, half bewildered.

"Here, read and understand," said Kharapet, spreading out the letters with trembling hands. "See what a devilish device! She, so proud, so cold, she has given herself to some beggar; she has refused me for some scoundrel who dared not ask for her openly. We will have her back, shall we not? and punish both. What is your law for such an offence, Harding? foolishness, I doubt not: a woman like that should not live;" and he suddenly burst into Hindoostanee, speaking with vehemence in broken sentences, gasping as if for breath between them, as though under the influence of furious passion.

Even Mr. Harding's attention was diverted for a moment from the papers before him. "Gad! you have lost your senses, Kharapet, you don't know what you are talking about; pull yourself together, for this is a nasty business. Here, let me understand."

Thus admonished, Kharapet seemed to recover some of his habitual self‑control, though his voice still trembled, and his tongue seemed parched. He explained how these letters had just arrived, and that the one enclosed had been forwarded to C—— by Miss Stretton. Mr. Harding now began to peruse them, and his wife, thrilling with anxiety, leant over his shoulder as he had resumed his seat. Kharapet paced the room, striving to master his agitation.

"It is pretty clear then," said Harding, looking up, "that Stasie disappeared on the 28th, this day week, and has not since been heard of. Now she didn't go alone : the thing has been well planned. She has got a week the start of us; it will be devilish hard to track her ; our only chance is knowing the train she travelled by. The guard may have noticed who met her. We must apply to the police. The question is, Who is the man ? Have you any idea?" turning sharply on his wife.

"I have no reason to suspect any one," she said nervously. "Could it be that—that Mr. Pearson ?"

Mr. Harding shook his head. "He need not have run off with her. We could not have refused him if *she* consented ; it would have been a suitable marriage." Kharapet murmured something. "No, that's not the man. Whom else did she know?" continued Harding, "your cousin Brooke, eh, Livy? He is unlikely to do anything disreputable. He would have asked openly; no, it is some secret disgraceful affair." Here poor Miss Stretton came in, her bonnet awry, her shawl half off, and sinking on the sofa proceeded to drown herself in tears.

"I am convinced that the dear child had no attachment whatever; she was the essence of all that is modest and correct. She has been taken away by stratagem: I saw there was a dark man bent on working her evil."

"That is all trash," replied Harding rudely. "What do *you* think?" to his wife.

"I do not know what to think or whom to suspect, but I am afraid Stasie has gone of her own free will."

"At any rate, she has done for herself. We cannot break the marriage now. It's a devil of a business. You don't think it's Brooke's doing, do you?"

"It is the last thing I should accuse him of," cried Mrs. Harding warmly; "besides, he has been away in Paris for quite three weeks."

"Are you sure of that?"

"Yes; Mr. Robinson had a letter from him from Paris the other day."

"Send Robinson a line asking for the letter," cried Mr. Harding: "ask him to come up;" then, looking hard at his wife, "If I thought you had any hand in this, by ——, you'd find out *how* angry I'd be."

In all her deep distress for her friend, Mrs. Harding remembered the task she had undertaken, and, looking straight into her husband's eyes, she said quietly and firmly, "I should do what I thought right, irrespective of *your* anger. However, I can truly say that I have not the smallest reason to suppose Dr. Brooke capable of such a breach of propriety."

Harding's eyes fell, and he then exclaimed, "Why, what dolts we have all been! Here, this letter may throw some light on the matter," and he picked up the one which had been returned to Miss Stretton, and unhesitatingly opened it. "By Jove!" he exclaimed in great surprise, "it is from that scamp young Mathews, and here's a bill on Grey, Hughes, and Co. for £15; it is dated from Shanghai." He proceeded to read—

"My dear Stasie—We are only just in

port after a splendid voyage. Not a soul among
the passengers afforded me an opportunity of
proving my skill; but a couple of the crew were
obliging enough to be ill, and I cured them first-
rate. I have made friends with the captain,
who has relations here, and they have asked me
to stay with them. I am to draw my pay to-
morrow, so I'll send £15, as a first instalment off
my debt to you. I'm not good at sentiment,
but I believe you've been the making of me, and
I'll never forget it. You take care of yourself,
Stasie, for you are an uncommon nice girl; don't
you be imposed upon. I don't think much of
that long-legged doctor; you've rather a fancy
for him, or I'm much mistaken. I'll be right
glad when I know you are safe out of the clutches
of those greedy sneaks the executors. Wouldn't
they like to pocket your cash and send you about
your business, in spite of their white chokered
respectability? I declare, if we were not so like
brother and sister, I'd marry you myself, just to
look after you. I have to write home, so must
stop. God bless you! may you fall into the
hands of as good a fellow as yourself is the prayer
of yours ever,   ROBERT MATHEWS."

" The vulgar, impudent, young blackguard," cried Mr. Harding indignantly, " what do you say to that, ma'am ? " to poor Miss Stretton, as the most helpless object on which to pour the vials of his wrath. " There is a nice intimate friend for a young lady. I don't think we need doubt now about her being too delicate to run off of her own free will."

" I will . . ne . . ver give up my . . faith in that swe . . et girl," sobbed Aunt Clem, " though what is to become of me I know not."

" If you had looked after her a little sharper ——began Mr. Harding, folding up Bob's bill, and proceeding to put it into his pocket-book.

" Pardon me, Mr. Harding ! " said Kharapet, almost restored to himself at the sight of this appropriation, " *I* have the best right to that. I redeemed the jewels with my own money, and —you had better give it to me."

" Pooh, nonsense ; we'll place it to the account, and you can have your interest."

Kharapet objected, and a warm dispute would have raged had not Mr. Robinson been announced.

" I have just met your messenger, Mrs. Harding, and have come in to answer in person. Why, what is the matter?"

It was soon explained, and the little man was deeply distressed. He was quite sure Brooke was not the partner of Miss Verner's flight, though he fancied his friend was a good deal impressed by that young lady's charms. As to the note, he had unfortunately torn it up. There was nothing in it, but he quite well remembered that the post-mark was Paris, October 28. After this came a great confusion of tongues, and Mrs. Harding at length avowed her leaning to the theory of Brooke being the delinquent. She thought his great anxiety about Stasie's health was more than that of an acquaintance; in short, she knew he would have gladly tried to win her, but feared she did not favour him; then the hint in Bob Mathews' letter, and——she could not tell why, but the conviction grew upon her, she had often thought Dr. Brooke unnecessarily alarmed about Miss Verner's health.

Kharapet turned many colours while Mrs. Harding spoke, and a silence ensued, broken by an occasional sob from Miss Stretton, who saw all her fair hopes of the future shivered and laid low. " I cannot believe Dr. Brooke guilty of such reckless impropriety," said Mr. Harding, " I think it more in that smart young lancer's line. Let us send over to Hounslow and ascertain his whereabouts, and now there is nothing left but to put the matter in the hands of the police. The mischief is done ; we can but do our best to save the property. You had better come with me, Kharapet."

That individual rose mechanically from the chair into which he had subsided—pale, limp, crest-fallen.

" Do, do take some refreshment, my dear sir," cried Miss Stretton, faithful to the last, " you have had a great shock, and you need support." But Kharapet was too far gone to heed anything, till Mrs. Harding, struck by his exhausted look, seconded Miss Stretton's proposition. Then the gentlemen departed on their rather hopeless errand, and Mrs. Harding kindly insisted on poor distracted Aunt Clem spending the rest of the day with her.

.   .   .   .   .

But the search was difficult ; so much time had been gained by the fugitive that her traces were lost.

Meantime, the days flew fast for the newly-married pair. The strange sweetness of finding herself the object of passionate affection, and, at length, bound by the ties of duty as well as preference, lent a new aspect to life in Stasie's eyes. Yet she could not feel quite at rest until all was known to the few friends she valued so highly, and more than once she hinted to her husband that it would be well to return to London and get through the bad quarter of an hour which awaited them, as quickly as possible.

But Brooke could not bring himself to curtail the delicious interval by a moment. He had never dreamed of anything half so delightful as this close and loving intercourse with a heart and mind so fresh, so keen to perceive, to enjoy, to learn, ready to look up to and believe in him, yet never losing their individuality. It seemed to bring back the brightness and vitality of his own boyhood, without lessening the strength and richness accumulated by matured nature.

To avoid the roving English who abound at all times and seasons in Europe's fairest capital, Brooke had selected an old-fashioned hotel near the

Luxembourg, where everything was thoroughly French. He himself often made excursions to the more cosmopolitan side of the Seine, to get books, English papers, etc., but Stasie kept out of sight in the old Fabourg.

One morning (for Brooke considered that the safest time of day) as he was leaving Gagliani's, intending to cross the Tuileries gardens to the bridges, he ran against a very English-looking Englishman—clean shaved, with snowy linen, and correct travelling costume. The gentleman started back and begged pardon. To Brooke's surprise he recognised Mr. Percy Wyatt. Our doctor was a man of prompt decision; he immediately raised his hat, saying, "Mr. Percy Wyatt, I think?"

"Yes," said that gentleman blandly; "I am sure I know you quite well, but at this moment I cannot remember your name."

"I have only had the pleasure of meeting you twice," replied Brooke, "and in your busy life you see so many that I do not expect you to remember me. I am a little better known to Lady Elizabeth. Allow me to introduce myself—Dr. Brooke, —th Dragoons."

" Very happy, I am sure."

" Is Lady Elizabeth in Paris ? "

" Yes, yes ; we arrived the night before last from Istria. Most interesting country. We have had some very curious experiences ! The abuses there are frightful, most frightful. I mean to expose them thoroughly."

" Ah ! a fatiguing journey for Lady Elizabeth."

" No doubt, but her energy is amazing, quite amazing."

" I should like to do myself the honour of calling, if you think Lady Elizabeth would be disposed to receive me."

" Oh, certainly ; by all means," said Mr. Wyatt, who was never quite certain of his ground among his wife's many favourites, and was not sure as to Brooke's standing. He might be the last A1 ; and at any rate there could be no harm in admitting a good-looking, well-bred man. " I am just returning to Meurice's (we always put up at Meurice's) ; come with me. She will be de-lighted to see you."

Brooke very readily complied.

Her ladyship was not in the little salon when they ascended to Mr. Wyatt's suite of apartments,

and Brooke lost no time in opening up his subject.

"I want to ask Lady Elizabeth's permission
to present my wife to her. We are here on our
wedding trip."

"Oh, indeed! I was not aware. Very interesting, I am sure."

"The fact is," resumed Brooke, "the young
lady is an orphan and was rather peculiarly situated. Her guardian at a distance, a dangerous
rival to be circumvented; so I persuaded her to
dispense with consents, and escape with me."

"Indeed! Very romantic! very interesting!
Lady Elizabeth will be deeply——Oh, here she
is! My dear! this is a friend of yours—Dr.
Brooke—who is anxious to know how you have
borne the fatigue of our adventurous journey."

"Ah! Dr. Brooke," said her ladyship graci-
ously, "I am very glad to see you! I am sure
it is a marvel that I am alive! I am going to
write my experiences, which I am sure Bentley
will be delighted to publish. I have made copi-
ous notes," etc. etc.

Brooke listened patiently with profound attention for nearly half an hour, at the end of which

time her ladyship being exhausted for the moment, Mr. Wyatt put in his word.

"Our friend here has been committing matrimony since we had the pleasure of seeing him— ran away with a young lady, to escape a dangerous rival! Quite a romance of the nineteenth century."

"How shocking!" cried Lady Elizabeth, with a winning smile. "I should not have believed it of you, Dr. Brooke. I hope she has a large fortune!"

"I am not sure what she has, Lady Elizabeth. But I should like to ensure your acquaintance and friendly offices. Your backing up would be of great importance, I need not say."

"Indeed! you overestimate my influence," cried Lady Elizabeth; "but such as it is it will, I am sure, be at your service when you have told me a few particulars."

"These you have a right to ask," returned Brooke, smiling. "My wife is an orphan, she has no near relative. Her guardian, a man of high position, who is necessarily almost a stranger to her, was away, we scarce knew where. She was persecuted by a man she did not like. The

time of my return to my regiment was drawing
near, so, with much difficulty, I persuaded her to
run away with me."

Lady Elizabeth listened with deep attention,
a light dawning on her as Brooke spoke. " Pray,
are you not some relation of Mrs. Harding's ? "
she asked, as he paused.

" I am her first cousin."

" Then you have run away with Stasie Verner?"
cried her ladyship, clasping her hands together.

" I have."

" With my ward ! This is most extraordinary
— most reprehensible — most — most — really,
words fail me ! And, great heavens ! what an
additional load of work and worry it will lay on
my already overburdened shoulders. It is most
inconsiderate, to say the least, and—and——"
cried Mr. Wyatt.

" My dear sir, do not worry yourself unnecessarily," said Brooke with quiet decision. " Stasie
has been my wife for nearly three weeks. Nothing can undo that. Give your consent, and all
difficulty will be at an end. Tie up my wife's
fortune as you like, so long as she has the benefit
of it, backed up by you, the executors cannot

object, and you will find that in the end I have saved instead of given you trouble."

Mr. Wyatt was much struck by the arguments adduced by Brooke, who proceeded to lay his own position and prospects before the philanthropic M.P. Lady Elizabeth, after some demur occasioned by backward glances to her favourite of last season, was caught by the glow of Brooke's language and the force of his representation. Both being mainly influenced by the fact that nothing now could undo the marriage; so at last Mr. Wyatt, having stipulated for the most careful detail in the post-nuptial settlement, agreed to withdraw all opposition. Whereupon Brooke, determined to strike while the iron was hot, persuaded the guardian to write his consent, addressed to Mr. Harding, which Brooke accompanied by a friendly letter from himself.

Stasie had been wondering at her husband's prolonged absence, and even began to hope that nothing unpleasant had occurred, when he entered, looking so radiant that she sprang up to meet him, exclaiming, "Who have you seen?"

"My darling," cried Brooke, throwing his arms round her, "sit down and write to Livy

Harding and Aunt Clem as fast as you like. I have been spending the morning with Mr. Wyatt and Lady Elizabeth. He has not only given his consent, but written it; and that limb of Satan, the executor, is fairly checkmated.

. . . . .

With virtue rewarded and vice defeated, if not punished, the story ought to end. Very little remains to tell.

Of course the bride and bridegroom returned to London, to wait the conclusion of legal matters before going to Italy for the remainder of winter.

Aunt Clem again retired into "furnished apartments," but they were neither mean nor uncomfortable; and she frequently observed to her female friends, of whom quite an agreeable circle gathered round her, "that a sweeter or more distinguished young creature than her niece, Mrs. Brooke, did not exist—and grateful too. She has never forgotten how faithfully I stood by her in very trying circumstances."

Mr. Harding found he had to reckon with a very friendly inquisitor when matters came to be investigated, and the little errors he had committed, in his efforts to enrich his young friend, were overlooked. On the whole, Stasie's fortune was nearly intact.

On one point Brooke was inflexible. He would not permit Kharapet to enter his wife's presence. Indeed, he wrote what Kharapet told Miss Stretton in confidence was a most unchristian and uncharitable letter which, out of consideration to Stasie's husband, he (Kharapet) had destroyed. In short, the gentle Syrian thought it well to avoid his former beloved niece, and to find that pressing business demanded his presence in Bombay.

A few days before Dr. and Mrs. Brooke were to start on their southward journey, he was reading the *Times* after breakfast, when he uttered an exclamation, and called to his wife, " Look at this, Stasie ! "

She came, and leaning upon his shoulder, read as follows, under the head of " Police Intelligence : "

" Thames Street.—Inspector Moule of the C Division attended to explain to the magistrate the circumstances attending the death of a Hindoo, who was yesterday seized with strong convulsions in a lane near Wapping, and who died while being removed to the infirmary. The man

was well dressed, and had a considerable sum—
over fifty pounds—sewn up in his waistband.
In a pocket-book was a certificate of good char-
racter, and a recommendation to captains of ves-
sels trading to Bombay, of the bearer, Bhoodhoo,
a native of that town, signed by Mr. Harding, a
gentleman well known in the city, and Mr. Hormuz
Kharapet, whose interesting speeches in favour of
extending English protection to the Christians of
Syria, at the meeting in favour of that project,
may be remembered. Epilepsy, conjoined with a
weak heart, is supposed to have been the cause of
death. The magistrate directed that the gentlemen above mentioned should be communicated
with, in order to obtain their directions respecting
the disposal of the poor man's money."

Brooke looked at his wife significantly, and
said in a low voice, " The dead tell no tales."

Stasie's lip quivered, and putting her arms
round his neck, they exchanged a long, silent
embrace.

THE END.

Printed by R. & R. CLARK, *Edinburgh.*

www.ingramcontent.com/pod-product-compliance
Lightning Source LLC
Chambersburg PA
CBHW020950030726
47496CB00005B/1434